WAGNER
AND HIS
OPERA

Previous page:
Richard Wagner,
gazing at new worlds
to conquer. From a
print published in
New York, 1882.

The World of Opera

Wagner

by Rowland Cotterill

OMNIBUS PRESS

British Library Cataloguing in
Publication Data:
A catalogue record for this book is
available from the British Library.

Copyright © Rowland Cotterill 1996
Order No.OP47817
ISBN 0-7119-5501-8

First published in softback in the UK
in 1996 by Omnibus Press
(a division of Book Sales Limited),
8/9 Frith Street, London W1V 5TZ.

Exclusive Distributors:
Book Sales Limited,
8/9 Frith Street, London W1V 5TZ.
Music Sales Corporation,
257 Park Avenue South, New York,
NY10010, USA.
Music Sales Pty Limited,
120 Rothschild Avenue, Rosebery,
NSW2018, Australia.

To the Music Trade only:
Music Sales Limited,
8/9 Frith Street, London W1V 5TZ.

Cover designed by Michael Bell Design.
Text edited and designed by
Three's Company, 5 Dryden Street,
London WC2.
Cover photograph courtesy of Pictorial Press.

Printed and bound in Great Britain by
Butler & Tanner Ltd, Frome and London

Contents

Picture acknowledgments
Picture research by Image Select
Elizabeth Davis
Alexander Goldberg

Picture credits
Art Resource/Snark International: pp.
135, 155
Catherine Ashmore/Zoë Dominic
Photographs: p. 145
Clive Barda: pp. 93, 113
Hulton Deutsch: p. 119
Image Select: pp. 9, 13, 27, 29, 33,
35, 37, 43, 47, 49, 56-57, 63, 65, 71,
77, 87, 91, 97, 98, 99, 101, 103, 111,
115, 117, 133, 139, 141, 143, 151
The Mansell Collection: p. 127
Popperfoto: pp. 3, 11, 45, 121
Ann Ronan at Image Select: pp. 1, 15,
21, 51, 85, 106, 107, 113, 137, 147

Foreword

Wagner's operas and music-dramas remain impressively prominent in the repertoires of the opera-houses of the world, and the impact of his music upon his younger contemporaries and successors was immense. No excuse is needed for another short book which attempts some new assessments of his achievement.

I have tried to say a little more than is usually said concerning Wagner's place in the traditions of German theatre, as well as in German and European opera. I suggest that Wagner's misunderstandings, as well as understandings, of Schopenhauer are revealing and creatively fruitful. It seems worthwhile to include a fairly detailed account of the plots of the mature dramas; in many cases they represent unique Wagnerian combinations and developments of traditional narratives not previously drawn together, and thus form important material for the study of Wagner's thought. In the analyses I have tried to balance musical and literary-dramatic considerations.

The *Ring* merits a chapter to itself, separate from the analyses of component music-dramas. I take the *Ring* and *Tristan und Isolde*, works immensely different from each other, to mark the summit of Wagner's achievement. My view of *Die Meistersinger* is critical to the point of mild hostility, which can coexist with affection and even love, and is meant to stimulate new discussion. I emphasise both continuities and differences between Wagnerian theory and Wagnerian practice. I see the survival of musical, theatrical and conceptual elements from the early to the mature and the late Wagner as both demonstrable and, on the whole, valuable. I sense that the Wagner who emerges from these interpretations is marked out less by his own ideal of artistic unity than by the Brechtian touchstone – 'separation of the elements'.

My account of Wagner's life contains no new facts, though a number of possibly new interpretations and opinions, some of them implicit in its organisation. I have tried to make use of recent scholarly work here. An admirable source, for biography and everything else, is *The Wagner Compendium*, edited by Barry Millington (Thames and Hudson, London, 1992). All interested in Wagner will be in its debt. Some of the ideas in this book were floated in classes which I led, nearly two decades ago, under the auspices of the University of Birmingham's Extramural Department.

I am grateful to Tim Dowley for his suggestion that I write this book, and thus give those ideas a slightly less transient form. I owe a great debt, and great pleasure, to countless musical interpreters of Wagner – above all, like many of my contemporaries, to those performing in the English National Opera productions of the 1970s under Sir Reginald Goodall – and to friends who have been fellow-interpreters of those interpretations: Rosa Dover, Tony Phelan and above all my wife Helen Lloyd. She and my two children have endured high levels of tension during the writing of this book; and Marie Walsh has tirelessly read my writing and listened to my voice. To them all, my thanks.

Rowland Cotterill
December 1995

Chapter 1

Richard Wagner

Ludwig Geyer, 1779-1821; actor, painter, friend of Wagner's parents, sometimes believed to be Wagner's father.

The house in which Wagner was born, in the Bruhl, Leipzig.

Wilhelm Richard Wagner was born in Leipzig on May 22nd 1813. He was the ninth child born to his mother, Johanna Rosine, and the last issue of her marriage to Carl Friedrich Wagner – if indeed he was Carl Friedrich's son. Carl Friedrich died six months after Richard's birth. Johanna was financially

protected by an actor, Ludwig Geyer, to whom she became engaged in February 1814 and married in August. Geyer, Richard's effective father (until 1827 the boy was known as Richard Geyer), had already been a close friend and lodger of the family. Johanna took the baby Richard from Leipzig on an extended visit to Geyer, in Teplitz, two months after his birth. The journey was over 100 miles each way and through country made dangerous by war: Johanna's readiness to face its risks is the main, though insufficient, evidence to support the argument for Geyer's paternity of Richard. Richard felt uncertain of his father's identity; his operas and music–dramas abound in male children without visible or acknowledged fathers – Siegmund, Siegfried, Tristan and Parsifal – or, like Lohengrin and Hagen, committed to fathers who remain largely absent.

Carl Friedrich, employed as an actuary in the police service, was a lover of the theatre (and possibly of an actress, Friederike Worthon) – hence Geyer's friendship with the family. Geyer had been a law student and a keen painter and amateur actor before, at twenty-six, turning professional. Wagner the composer thus inherited, directly and/or from his early surroundings, the sense of theatre as a natural milieu for the imagination. He also inherited a sense of life determined by enthusiasms and desires rather than obligations or financial necessities.

Wagner's central theoretical writings were to uphold the ideal of the *Gesamtkunstwerk* – a work drawing together into an organic unity the products and skills of different forms of art. But his own development was to proceed less towards any unity, of his own many artistic skills and aptitudes, than along paths encouraged and dictated by his genius for improvisation. He was also to be guided by confidence in his ability quickly to master, and even to reform and regenerate, any artistic discipline to which he might wish, or need, to turn his hand. Parts of his family inheritance may perhaps have lain behind this remarkable talent for self–fashioning.

He may also have taken from them some sense that 'identity' was an area of mystery, secrecy and suffering. His uncertainty about his paternity was refracted through his belief that Geyer was of Jewish descent: in terms of Wagner's later scurrilous polemic against Jews, Judaism and the Jewish 'race', this would have been for him a source of bitter irony and vulnerability. Geyer was in fact, though Wagner never knew this, descended from Protestant ancestors.

Wagner's mother did have a family secret. She had been seduced, at the age of fifteen or sixteen, in 1790 by Prince Constantin of Saxe–Weimar–Eisenach. He provided her with a lodging in Leipzig, an allowance and a basic education: the allowance ended with his early death in 1793. The prince's elder

Johanna Wagner, the composer's mother; mother of ten children, mistress of a prince. Water-colour by August Bohm, Leipzig, 1839.

brother was famous as the patron and friend of Goethe. Of Wagner's dramatic heroines, Senta, Elsa, Sieglinde and Eva are compulsively attracted to men of glamorous though undefined family prestige: in Eva's case this involves also the attraction exerted by creative genius. Such relationships, in the operas, are blighted by fears of treachery or limited by demands of propriety.

Wagner seems to have admired his mother, until her death in 1848, without ever feeling quite sure of her admiration or affection. She loved talking to him about poetry, music and painting, but hated his fascination with the theatre. His letters to her were warm but rare; writing in 1842 to his sister Cäcilie and her husband, he spoke of her 'remarkable penchant for misrepresenting and distorting everything'.

Napoleon, the supreme self–fashioner of the period before Wagner, played a less shadowy role than Goethe's in Wagner's infancy. After the disastrous retreat of the French imperial army from Moscow, Napoleon was threatened, in 1813, by a coalition of Russia and Prussia. With the support of the Confederacy of the Rhine, he occupied Dresden in March. Dresden was the capital of the King of Saxony (Friedrich), who fled to Prague. Napoleon was victorious in a series of battles between May and August, the months of Wagner's birth and earliest infancy (and of his mother's journey across country beset by armies). In October Napoleon was defeated at the Battle of Leipzig, and deserted by the Saxon troops: the king of Saxony did not return till May 1815, and the destiny of the kingdom was for some time uncertain.

The constitutions of German states, and the map of central Europe, were to be changed, or exposed to change, a number of times in Wagner's life, with his participation or approbation: and his attitudes to France and French culture, often overtly hostile, were in fact as complex as those of most German thinkers, artists and publicists, for whom the French Revolution, and its power to disturb inherited structures of law and society, was at once a stimulus and an alien threat.

Wagner's education
Like Napoleon, Wagner was a notably short adult, and conscious of the fact; his head was notably large. In childhood he was sickly, pale and slim. At the age of seven he took piano lessons from Christian Wetzel, a pastor at Possendorf near Dresden, with whom he was at that time lodged. Geyer died in 1821; he was fond of the boy, whether step–son or son, and had hoped to launch him into a successful creative life, probably as a painter. On his deathbed he is said to have heard him playing the piano and wondered aloud whether he might not after all become a musician. Richard's older sisters, Rosalie, Luise and Klara, were all to fulfil the promise of their names, drawn from heroines of dramas by Schiller, the greatest playwright hitherto in the German language, in stage careers. Richard never pursued this path, despite early verbal fluency shown in wit, quarrels and family diplomacy: but his readings (and sometimes vocal performances) of his operas were to prove powerful demonstrations of his ability as a theatrical artist.

In December 1822 he began attending the Kreuzschule in Dresden, still as Richard Geyer. When his family moved to Prague in 1826, where Rosalie had achieved success in the theatre, he remained in Dresden. On a school trip to Leipzig in

Adolf Wagner, the composer's uncle; scholar and free-thinker, book-collector and friend of famous writers.

1827 he met Adolf Wagner, brother of Carl Friedrich, a gifted linguist and a friend or acquaintance of leading German writers of earlier generations – Goethe and Schiller, Fichte and Tieck. Adolf Wagner appreciated plays and literature while disliking the theatre, a not unusual attitude for a Romantic and a German intellectual. The significance of Richard Wagner's time with his uncle may have been increased by his acquisition, on the same visit, of Geyer's library. Wagner's movements, poverty and chronic indebtedness throughout the 1830s left him little chance of accumulating books: but in Dresden again, on a regular salary, in the middle 1840s, he formed the nucleus of the collection which made him one of the best–read composers in music history. In our century Michael Tippett, similarly eclectic in musical style and reading tastes, offers some comparison.

In December 1827 Richard returned to Leipzig, where in the next month he entered the Nikolaischule. He now took the name Richard Wagner. (It is not clear why; possibly out of admiration for his uncle Adolf, possibly to mark a new, distinct identity, as student and artist.) Creative writing excited him more than academic tasks: in 1828 he wrote his first work of art, a tragedy *Leubald*. In order to write music for it he studied a harmonic manual, and in the autumn began lessons with a Leipzig musician, Christian Gottlieb Müller. The lessons lasted for three years. Though dismissed by Wagner in his fascinating and tendentious autobiography, *My Life*, begun in 1865, they seem likely to have provided him, at an impressionable age, with the crucial basis of the very competent technique shown in his compositions of the early 1830s.

Wagner clung to the notion of himself as essentially self-taught. It would be nearer the mark to see him as remarkably swift to grasp the whole basis of contemporary musical language – above all, the subtle interdependence upon one another of rhythm, melody, harmony, tonality and form. In this, as in many ways, his gifts disposed him towards a fluent conservatism of style: his revolutionary energies were more often evoked by the demands of a crisis.

Adolescent years at the Nikolaischule included important experiences: the reading of Karl Friedrich Becker's *History of the World*, the copying of scores by major composers and the transcription of Beethoven's 'Choral' Symphony for piano, the composition of piano and chamber music (now lost), and an infatuation for the daughter of a Jewish banker. In *My Life* he claimed that another experience was even more powerful – a performance of Beethoven's *Fidelio* in which the title role was sung by the dramatic soprano Wilhelmine Schröder–Devrient. It is true that both singer and composer were crucial to Wagner's growth into maturity as an opera composer, but no such Leipzig performance is on record at the time he specified. Again it seems that the middle-aged Wagner needed the security conferred by a sense of his earlier maturation as guided by inevitable logic, rather than (as it was) by chance and choice.

The Paris revolution of July 1830 prompted riots among the student body at Leipzig – until the city authorities gave them arms against the workers. Wagner, now officially a student of music at the Thomasschule, joined with them: he may have remembered this moment of ambiguous effectiveness when he constructed the roles of the nobles, first leading, and then opposing, revolt, in *Rienzi* nearly ten years later. The major Polish revolt of 1830, against the Russians, was to provide the peg for Wagner's *Polonia* overture of 1836, and for him as for many Europeans the emotions and ideas generated by 1830 were to be remembered, and to bear fruit, in 1848 and 1849.

The earliest works

Wagner's earliest surviving orchestral works include a number of overtures – others are lost. Such works allowed him to demonstrate control of the basic elements of musical style, ability to write for the forces of the early-Romantic orchestra (with brass and percussion frequently prominent), and imagination capable of evoking extra-musical references and dramatic contexts. Overtures thus offered a link, as, in his view, did his entire mature musico-dramatic achievement, between 'symphony' and 'opera'.

In 1831 Wagner took some lessons with a new music teacher, Christian Theodor Weinlig, the Kantor of the church of St Thomas and, in this post, a successor at a century's distance of J.S. Bach. Early fruits of these lessons were two full-length (and surviving) piano sonatas, in B flat and in A, recognisably modelled on the clear formal articulation and fluent pianistic virtuosity of Beethoven's early sonatas. In 1832 he completed a Symphony in C – this, his only symphony, he never disavowed, and was moved to hear, in a special privately-prepared performance, fifty years later: again comparisons with Beethoven's early and middle work are revealing and not unflattering. In the same year he planned a three-act opera, *Die Hochzeit* (The Wedding), and began its text and music. He abandoned these in spring 1833: it is interesting that he had expected to be capable of providing his own text.

But these student years, as well as leaving him with student debts, had tilted the balance of his energies towards music. Theatrical employment was an obvious possibility as a career: his brother Albert, with whom he stayed in January 1833, was a singer and actor at the Würzburg theatre, and enabled Richard to get a post as chorus-master there. At Würzburg Wagner com-

Carl Maria von Weber, 1786-1826, composer of *Der Freischütz, Oberon* and *Euryanthe*.

pleted his first complete opera, *Die Feen* (The Fairies). He also trained chorus and solo singers in operas by the leading French and German composers of the time – and of the preceding generation – Cherubini and Rossini, Herold, Auber and Meyerbeer, Weber and Marschner. More than ten years earlier the boy Wagner had joined in the enthusiasm with which Weber's *Der Freischütz* was received on its first performance in Dresden: back in Dresden in 1844 he was to compose music for a ceremony in which the remains of the older composer, who had died in 1826, were transported to Dresden from London. The brief Würzburg year played a major part in determining the operatic lineage of Wagner's early mature style.

15

Romantic and nationalist

In his theoretical writings, Wagner was concerned not only to set the events of his own life in an order humanly plausible and dramatically persuasive, but to fulfil the same obligation towards the processes of artistic history. He meant to display his achievement in opera as the flowering of a distinctive 'German' tradition, and to indicate the limitations, misunderstandings and constraints under which that tradition had laboured. He traced these limitations to the subjugation of German opera by the influences of Italian and, especially, French opera. Such an interpretation, though self–serving, is intelligent and plausible. It is also an example of something that Wagner took for granted: Romantic historicist nationalism.

'Historicism', in modern academic usage, often indicates a mode of thought emphasizing the differences between past and present, and between one past and another. Such 'historicism' is sceptical about claims for continuity, whether of human nature, cultural assumptions or socioeconomic circumstances. Nineteenth-century historians are also often thought of as 'historicist'. Their polar difference from modern cultural historians was rooted in philosophical reflection, which seemed to legitimise certain beliefs concerning human and national identity, and invest them with the force of the most up-to-date conceptual advances.

According to such views, human individual identity was neither immutable nor liable to sudden arbitrary change, but was organically coherent and, under favourable circumstances, likely to change by growing – as a flower grows. Growth was pre-eminently to be found in the power of self-expression; self-expression could be identified at every level of social life, thus rendering uncertain the prominent eighteenth-century divisions between 'public' and 'private' life; but its outstanding instances were to be sought in the lives – that is, the 'lives-and-works' – of creative artists. It is sometimes suggested that 'Romantic art' can be defined by an artist's highly-developed self-obsession, or a preoccupation with 'sincerity' (considered as truth to oneself); or that Romantic artists lived lives enacting, or seeking to anticipate, the themes of their art. Such notions all contain truth, but miss the heart of the positions they aim to represent, in failing to do justice to the concerns for 'growth', 'expression' and the complex connections between them, which did indeed activate very many major artists, in all fields, of the early nineteenth century.

Wagner was a Romantic, in this sense. He expected to grow in expressive power and energy, and could rightly have perceived himself to be growing, well in advance of making a commitment of himself to any specific medium of expression – words, drama, music or opera. He was also a Romantic historicist. He set his own growth in the context of the growth, in expressive power, of the media to which he was in due course concerned to contribute. And he was exercised – irritated, provoked and aroused – by finding himself, as he supposed, in a situation where these media, symphonic music and opera above all, were not commanding the attention of their audiences to the degree which their growth would have led one to expect. Hence his concern with himself was directed towards the interpretation and the promotion of his own expressive development, past and future: while his understanding of the power of musical and dramatic techniques was governed by a conception of the collective expressive growth, shared in principle by all humanity, which such techniques should be producing.

Wagner was also a nationalist. This would have both complicated and enriched any Romantic historicist programme; but German cultural nationalism was, and is, a particularly complicated set of propositions. Wagner's perceptions and applications of it showed it at its most plausible and its most tendentious. Hence his versions of cultural and operatic history require scrutiny even where they are most seemingly acceptable and self-evident.

'German culture' could reasonably be taken to include most literary and dramatic work written in the German language or its historical precursors. German scholars, as one might expect, were playing a highly important part by clarifying the history of Teutonic and Nordic languages, and by editing and publishing pre-Renaissance texts in those languages: their work was a crucial precondition, and an important influence, for Wagner's operas from the 1840s onwards. Artists in other media who were speakers of German could equally be placed within this context. But no major political unit commanded the allegiance, or defined the natural identity, of this group of artists. Until 1806 they were, and for long had been, dispersed across the vast number of mostly tiny political entities – kingdoms (like Saxony), free cities (like Augsburg), tiny dukedoms (like Weimar), bishoprics (like Cologne) and others – within the overall judicial realm of the Holy Roman Empire, ruled from Vienna. Moreover, 'German' artists might live outside Imperial territory, ruled by the king of Denmark or the Tsar of Russia, or inhabit a self-governing Swiss canton, or territories ruled by the kings of France or Poland. 'Germany' was a cultural not a political expression.

More precisely, it was a political aspiration, or threat. A future state embracing all or most German speakers might be centrally ruled from Vienna – but if so its rulers would be the Habsburg imperial family. They were Catholics, religiously distinct from, and formerly at war with, north German Protestants. They were also traditional dynasts, defined by family continuity rather than any popularly-conferred legitimacy, and sovereigns over many non-German-speaking peoples – Serbs, Croats, Slovenians, Magyars, Czechs, Slovaks, Ruthenians, Italians and Poles. Such a state could not provide any reliable focus for the 'German' culture on which national aspirations most obviously focused. But any alternative German capital would compete with the traditions of Viennese centrality and the claims of all other historic German cities. Napoleon's abolition of the Holy Roman Empire in 1806, and the relative simplification of central European political geography achieved in 1815 by the Congress of Vienna, left the elements of the puzzle firmly in place. Some would-be German nationalists looked to Vienna: more looked to Prussia. Some were prepared to accept political multiplicity because it limited the powers of monarchic absolutism; others hoped for an enlightened monarch, supported by a vigorous large populace, capable of suppressing the pretensions of petty local princes.

A German culture

On these matters Wagner showed no consistent strong opinions. This indicates his intelligence, rather than that lack of any ultimate political interests which he, and others later, imputed to himself. He escaped the territory of the Russian Tsar, served the court of the King of Saxony, endured the surveillance of Imperial spies in Venice, enjoyed the patronage of the King of Bavaria, and hailed the triumph of Prussian arms and 'German' culture in 1871 after the Franco-Prussian war. *Die Meistersinger*, set in a less remote past than his other works, glorifies the culture of a free German city. But his defensible uncertainties about political forms went with a strong concern, offensive and defensive, for the integrity and continuity of German culture, and, in middle and later life, a virulent patrolling of the supposedly racial frontiers of German-ness against aliens without and within. The former category, given recent political and military history, mainly involved the French. The latter category meant Jews.

As a writer and dramatist he shared these concerns with very many German-speaking contemporaries and precursors. German dramatists, whether or not displaying allegiance to any recognisable programme of nationalism, had for several generations before the 1830s directed attention towards the issues with which it was concerned, and the complex political realities amidst which it arose. Kleist's *Der Prinz von Homburg* (The Prince of Homburg) could be taken as a glorification of the Prussian royal house. It was also a prescient indictment of a 'German' pattern of thought which set against each other

Romantic individualism and state absolutism, while implying their ultimate complementarity. Schiller's 'Wallenstein' trilogy linked the hesitations and torments of heroic self-consciousness to the relations between peoples, status groups and the house of Habsburg within the Empire. Goethe's early play *Götz von Berlichingen* glorified the life of the old free cities while indicating its inadequacy to modernity. The second part of his *Faust* presented the onset of modernity, in thought, politics and technology, as both a threat and a creative challenge. In plays written in the 1840s, Hebbel represented the emergence, from political confrontations, of new forms of spiritual life. Wagner was to read, dislike and perhaps be influenced by Hebbel's drama *Die Nibelungen* (The Nibelungs). His operas and music-dramas treat all the themes prominent in these earlier dramatic writers, while his use of drama as a vehicle for complex dialectical thought, at once about politics and evading its practical issues, could be fruitfully compared with both Goethe's and Hebbel's work.

Playwrights like these were also concerned to call into being the conditions within which their own work could be understood. A German national theatre might follow from a German national state, or might precede and help to create it. Recent criticism has illuminated the extent to which dramatists used deliberate anomalies of structure to generate the self-consciousness, and the mutual awareness, of audiences. Many such plays posed obvious material problems of staging – *Faust* more than any other. Few dramatists enjoyed the easy access to theatres or theatre companies which would have resolved such problems. In any case, tensions between dramatic purpose and theoretical convenience were often embraced as a stimulus to the immensely innovative developments of this period. In these ways, too, German dramatists offered Wagner a model and a challenge.

Wagner was prepared in the first half of his life to work in existing German theatres and eager to entrust his operas to them, but eventually embraced the virtual theatrical invisibility which, in the 1850s, his exile from German states imposed on him. He devoted himself to music-dramas likely to be published sooner than performed, and to prose essays which argued for the replacement, not only of existing operatic styles, but also of existing operatic audiences. Still, Wagner's situation was importantly different; he was both dramatist and musician.

Musical culture, frequently (at all times and in all places) characterized in terms of national or ethnic types, none the less evades the obvious national particularisms involved in verbal media: Italians, Germans and French might dislike each other's concertos, symphonies and dances, but could not point to any obvious features of incomprehensibility to excuse themselves from considering them. And Germans, under whatever political allegiance, had in the later eighteenth century developed to a level of overwhelming complexity and power certain forms of instrumental music. The 'meaning' of these forms, however defined or however indefinable, had least claim to be limited by cultural, political or national boundaries. Symphonic music – symphonies, sonatas, chamber music for strings and to some extent concertos – embodied the (arguable) pre-eminence of 'German' music, hence perhaps of German culture in general. It also, by a crucial paradox, suggested a linkage between a 'German' and a 'universal' or supra-national idea of music. These lines of thought converged in claims for the supremacy of music over other arts, and indeed all forms of human self-consciousness and self-representation, associated with the early-nineteenth-century German philosopher Arthur Schopenhauer, whose work was a major inspiration to Wagner in the 1850s.

Music, then, might embody the most impressive claims of German culture to universal recognition. By the same token the refusal, or merely partial acceptance, of German music by other, perhaps more securely entrenched, 'national' cultures could provoke nervousness and resentment. Such a situation was likely to arise where music and words joined; that is, in opera.

The evolution of opera

The earliest operas had been musical settings of Italian texts: the earliest public theatre for opera opened in Venice in 1637, and the most widely diffused operatic style of the eighteenth century could be traced back to principles laid down in the 1680s in Naples. 'Italy' was a 'geographical expression', and no more than Germany a unified national state. Such cultural unity as the Italian peninsula boasted lay in the gradual acceptance of one standard form of the written language (Tuscan). In turn, the unity of Italian musical culture was seen to rest in opera, where language, as well as music, transcended provincial frontiers.

Italian opera acquired, outside Italian-speaking territory, audiences which were polyglot (as, for example, in Vienna), or (as in London) drawn by virtuoso singers and expensive stage machinery. Its styles were widely recognised and sometimes parodied, as in Gay's *Beggar's Opera*. Their basis was the solo aria, often elaborate in vocal style, usually predictable in structure. Arias were separated by lightly-accompanied recitatives, in which the dramatic action was transacted, and more rarely by ensembles. The milieux of action were heroic, mythical or monarchic. Such opera provoked challenge from French styles, which became increasingly self-confident and flexible as the eighteenth century progressed.

French opera, unlike Italian, was an organized and highly regimented manifestation of a centralised culture. Courtly in its ori-

gins, it aspired to national acceptance. Musically it adopted features from Italian styles, and frequently employed Italian composers – Cherubini and Spontini, Rossini and Verdi, in the nineteenth century. Germans also made decisive contributions: Gluck, Meyerbeer (Wagner's helper, and bitter enemy), and, had he ever been accepted in Paris, Wagner himself. All these composers played important parts in the expansion of regular arias into unpredictable and dramatically flexible structures, in the linking of arias with each other, in the increasing dramatic importance of the chorus – which was a sign of new social mobility in operatic action – and in the ultimate collapsing of formal divisions between successive musico-dramatic events. Many of the achievements claimed by Wagner for his operas of the 1840s, and for German opera in general, were paralleled or anticipated in French opera, as he was certainly aware. French opera was arguably the dominant musical medium between 1750 and 1830, however much subsequent music historians might view this as the 'symphonic age'. But it remained merely a dominant medium. It was not, and could not be, a universal form.

German artists were rarely encouraged towards opera by their rulers. Some states and cities supported theatres where music punctuated, or accompanied, spoken drama. Operas in Italian dominated Viennese musical theatre in the later eighteenth century. Mozart's great Italian operas of the 1780s and early 1790s became, for German nineteenth-century opera, part of its own claimed pre-history. His *Die Entführung aus dem Serail* (The Abduction from the Harem) and *Die Zauberflöte* (The Magic Flute), from the same decade, more indisputably represent the earliest major landmarks in the performing tradition of German opera. Beethoven's *Fidelio* was claimed by Wagner as a decisive stimulus. But, up to and well beyond *Fidelio*, and Weber's *Der Freischütz*, 'German opera' remained the name less of a flourishing tradition than of a problematic challenge.

For one thing, the Italian and, especially, French traditions were already there: successful, influential and conceptually imposing. Any association of verbal drama with continuous music – no spoken words, little word-free music – often provoked philistine scorn or amusement. It invited cultural, historical and philosophical defence. It could inspire grandiose schemes of reform. The problems frequently seemed to hang on the question of the kind of text – its subject-matter, its style, its verbal and rhetorical forms – that musical rhetoric and form could accommodate or might require. In Italian and in French many successful, and some interestingly controversial, cases were available for debate. It might seem question-begging to argue for the viability of a new language's texts in relation to music.

Moreover, the universal claims and European triumphs of 'German' symphonic music encouraged notions of a predetermined division of cultural labour, between Italian-French opera and German instrumental music.

In any case, the works by Mozart, Beethoven and Weber mentioned above did not offer opera in the sense just described. They all employed significant, often extensive, spoken dialogue between musical 'numbers': only at some points (though crucial ones – above all in the 'finales' to acts) were distinct musical forms linked in a continuous musico-dramatic sequence. The importance of these German finales gives some legitimacy to the appropriation of Mozart's great Italian operas, with their magnificent extended finales, by a 'German' tradition. In modern performances the spoken dialogue is normally abbreviated; in recordings it has often been omitted. Such practices reflect an arbitrary belief in the indivisibility of 'operatic' style. But Wagner himself saw, in the use of spoken language, a prime mark of the immaturity of 'German opera'.

'Immaturity' rather than 'difference' – this line of thought indicates the pervasiveness of Romantic historicist nationalism, in Wagner and in many subsequent modes of argument about music and theatre. Wagner was convinced that music, and spoken words, each on their own, were deficient in the expressive powers which they gained, and communicated, when joined together. And, if the universalism of symphonic music challenged any narrowly local, or temporally or spatially limited, story-line, the solution lay in dramatic subjects as universal, and humanly unifying, as the music. 'German opera' might thus exchange its comparative immaturity for a role as unique exemplar of the full powers of musical theatre, and of German art in general. All this rested on the possibility of overcoming entrenched forms involving separation – separation of words from music, of one musical number from another, and ultimately of musical and verbal meaning from each other. And this argument in turn gained much of its power from the availability of obvious examples of such separation.

It would have been possible then, as it certainly is now, to see such 'separation of the elements' as a positive feature. The phrase 'separation of the elements' was coined by Brecht, in a polemic introduction to his only operatic libretto, *Der Aufstieg und Fall der Stadt Mahagonny* (The Rise and Fall of the City of Mahagonny), set by Kurt Weill. The scope of his argument embraces spoken theatre as well as opera. Brecht's own 'spoken' theatre normally includes enough songs to offer an example of a distinctive, defensible and 'German' form of music-theatre. Brecht may well in some measure have been attacking the theories and practices of Wagner's operas.

Wagner neglected, or never considered, the distinct musico-dramatic virtues of the separation advocated by Brecht, although he would have encountered it whenever he attended performances of German plays in German theatres. Like other German intellectuals of his time and since, he chose to consider such plays as directed towards readers, rather than towards the chances and risks of live performance. In consequence he perceived the requirements of 'German Opera', from his earliest work *Die Feen* onwards, as lying in 'union', 'assimilation' and 'unity'. Hence, paradoxically (and like many of his German intellectual contemporaries in other fields) he sought to create, and lead to artistic greatness, a German opera that would at last be as those of other nations.

Die Feen, Wagner's first opera, was not the first '*durchkomponiert*', or 'through-composed' German opera (that is, with the whole of its text set to continuous music). Its precursors in this respect include *Jessonda*, by Spohr, and Weber's musically impressive *Euryanthe*, both of which Wagner was to rehearse or conduct in the mid-1830s. *Die Feen* was probably the longest German opera of any kind composed up to that date. Wagner never heard it performed.

Die Feen: *plot*

Arindal is Prince of Tramond. Ada abducts him by magic into the realm of the King of the fairies: she will marry him on the condition of his willingness not to ask her identity for the next eight years. She is in fact half-mortal and half-fairy. He asks the forbidden question; the fairy realm vanishes. Gernot, who serves Arindal, and Morald, in love with his sister, persuade him to return to Tramond and succeed his dead father as king. Ada now urges these human claims upon him; she wishes to join him as his Queen, but is in turn subject to a fated penalty, for marriage to a mortal. Arindal passes through a series of trials. Ada appears to be imposing these, and has exacted from Arindal the promise that he will never curse her. He curses her: she reveals her own subjection to fate, and her penalty – a hundred years turned to stone. He goes mad, but follows her to the underworld where she is confined, and brings her back to life with music and song. In return he is made immortal. He leaves Tramond; he and Ada will reign in the realm of the fairies.

Die Feen: *commentary*

As in the case of all his later operas and music–dramas, Wagner wrote his own text. He followed, however, an existing play, by the eighteenth-century Venetian dramatist Carlo Gozzi, entitled *La donna serpente*. Some names of characters come from the planned, but never completed, *Die Hochzeit*.

The dramatic premise is the division between two realms, magical and human. The conduct of the drama, however, involves constant connections between the realms. Magic decrees bind both Ada the half-fairy and Arindal the mortal; a political obligation is perceived by Arindal and his courtiers but also by Ada. Ada and Arindal both infringe decrees and break oaths; both can and do undergo extreme suffering. Arindal is an inspired musician; Ada responds to his music.

The action, which logically could cease at many points, continues until not only an emotional resolution but a certain exhaustiveness of treatment is achieved. On the other hand the demands of the human kingdom of Tramond are ultimately relegated – it is in fairyland, but not on earth, that the happy couple will reign.

Arindal's sense of duty to his kingdom can be compared with the obligations acknowledged towards rulers by Tannhäuser, Lohengrin and Tristan, although none of them, of course, is of royal blood. Arindal's acceptance of negative obligations echoes Elsa's willingness not to ask Lohengrin's identity. More remotely, his double failure may be compared with the seeming inadequacies of the two 'positive' heroes of the *Ring*, Siegmund and Siegfried, and with the two trials of Parsifal, in the Grail hall and in Klingsor's garden. The power of human music to defy obstacles to love is in evidence in *Tannhäuser* and *Die Meistersinger*. Ada, though constrained at every turn by her divided condition and by 'fateful decrees', is of all Wagner's heroines the most active on her own behalf.

Major keys dominate the music, as in *Die Meistersinger*. Comic characters, with a distinctive musical idiom, are found alongside the potentially tragic leading roles – Wagner's next opera, *Das Liebesverbot*, is the closest parallel here. The conventional musical forms of recitative, aria and ensemble are used confidently and unselfconsciously; in the finale of the first act, seven solo voices are deployed with and against a chorus. Arindal's mad scene, in the final act, employs repeated chords of the diminished seventh to represent both the hero's anguish and the imagined noise of angry hunting dogs; the chord is prominent in Weber's *Der Freischütz*, where the 'Wolf's Glen' scene uses it in similar connections. It becomes a fundamental part of the extensions of harmonic language in Wagner's later work.

Connections between separate worlds, and the betrayal of such connections, are crucial to most of Wagner's dramas. *Undine*, an opera of 1816 by the German writer and composer E.T.A. Hoffmann, was one of the first influential treatments of such a theme in German musical theatre. Its water-spirit protagonist was acknowledged, immediately before his death, by Wagner as suggestively similar to the Rhinemaidens of the *Ring*.

Die Feen has claims to be regarded as a seminal work in Wagner's development. While closer in theme to Wagner's later works than either *Das Liebesverbot* or *Rienzi*, its resemblances to other German operas have perhaps contributed to its relative obscurity. Wagner came to represent his musical and dramatic evolution in a way that left him little room to acknowledge its many merits.

Chapter 2

Wanderer and Reformer

In January 1834 Wagner returned from Würzburg to Leipzig, where he spent the next six months. In this time he came under the influence of Heinrich Laube, who had been a friend of his family and was associated with the cultural, artistic and political movement known as 'Young Germany'. Laube published in June 1834 one of Wagner's earliest essays, entitled 'On German Opera'. In this Wagner praises the expressive qualities of Italian opera and criticizes the academic nature of German contributions to the genre – emphases significantly at

Wilhelmine Schröder-Devrient, 1804-1860; Wagner's inspiration as a singing actress, she created the roles of Adriano, Senta and Venus.

odds with his later views. Earlier in the year Wagner had admired the performance of Wilhelmine Schröder-Devrient in the part of Romeo in Bellini's opera on the Romeo and Juliet story, and this no doubt contributed to the argument of his essay. On a holiday in Bohemia Wagner sketched the prose version of what was to become the libretto for his second opera *Das Liebesverbot* (The Prohibition on Love). This opera, based on Shakespeare's play *Measure for Measure*, transfers the action from Vienna to Sicily. The enthusiasm for free love displayed in the opera relates to a 'Young German' desire to find 'Mediterranean' and even pagan values beneath the visible Catholic surface of Italian culture.

At the end of July 1834 Wagner was offered a post as musical director of a travelling theatre company run by Heinrich Bethmann. He was at first reluctant to undertake this job, feeling that the performers, in both dramatic and musical terms, were too run-down and unambitious to suit his own ideals. His mind changed when he was given a room in the same lodging as Christine Wilhelmine Planer. Minna Planer was three-and-a-half years older than Wagner. She had been abused, and subsequently abandoned, at the age of fifteen, and had had a child, Natalie, whom she brought up as her sister. Wagner was quickly drawn to her, and he took the post with Bethmann's company. At the start of August he made his debut with them as an opera conductor, with Mozart's *Don Giovanni*.

The company toured through many of the German-speaking theatres of central Europe. Wagner's work involved him in the composition of music for spoken theatre; for example in January 1835 he was writing music for a play *Columbus*. It also involved constant rehearsal of individual singers of widely differing vocal talents, and the pursuit of vocal ability outside the theatre company. It laid the foundations of Wagner's considerable gifts as a conductor in a wide range of operatic repertoire, gifts on which he was to rely on many subsequent occasions in his career.

But he also experienced the hostile audiences from which he was never to be entirely free. On one momentous occasion in April 1835 he at last had the chance to conduct Schröder-Devrient, whose performances he had so much admired. She enjoyed the experience of performing with him and offered him a benefit concert; but tickets sold poorly, and Wagner's own *Columbus* overture was received with derision, partly because of the immense size of the orchestra Wagner employed and the prominence within it of the brass and particularly the percussion sections.

In November 1835, Minna Planer left the company to take up an appointment in the prestigious Königstadt theatre in Berlin.

Minna Wagner, 1809-1866; Wagner's first wife.

Wagner's emotional reliance on her can be gauged from the stream of letters that he sent her over the next fortnight; she returned to Bethmann's company. Wagner himself was to visit Berlin in the spring of 1836 in an attempt to secure performances of the opera *Das Liebesverbot*. The work had already been premiered by Bethmann's company in Magdeburg, but the first and only performance was a fiasco. The company collapsed in bankruptcy in April. If Wagner was to remain in close contact with Minna he would have to depend upon the fortunes of her employment, and in July 1836 he followed her to the north-eastern German city of Königsberg. Here the only work available to him was as a conductor of church music. It was not until April 1837 that he was appointed musical director of the Königsberg theatre.

By this time Wagner had married Minna. Their marriage took place on 24th November 1836. It was preceded and followed by tensions and quarrels between the couple, concerning her sense of the high emotional demands he was placing upon her, and his views of her involvement with other singers and actors. In spring 1837 she did in fact leave Wagner to live with a merchant named Dietrich. Wagner pursued her, and eventually was reunited with her at her parents' home in Dresden.

The year at Königsberg had produced little from Wagner's pen in terms either of writing or musical composition, though two overtures composed in these years, the *Polonia* and *Rule Britannia*, merit more frequent performance than they have received. Their subjects indicate Wagner's liberal political sympathies at this time. Poland, a vast kingdom during the Middle Ages and Renaissance, had been progressively dismembered by the empires of Russia, Austria and Prussia. Briefly reconstituted by Napoleon, it had again been effectively eliminated from the map of Europe by the Congress of Vienna in 1815. A rising at the start of the 1830s had been repressed with great severity: many courts and cities of Western Europe resounded with the culture and the lamentations of Polish exiles, most famously Fryderyk Chopin. Wagner's *Polonia* could be taken as adding his voice to those of British and French liberal politicians calling for a break with the system of imperial hegemony in Eastern Europe. The *Rule Britannia* overture further indicates Wagner's sympathies with Western, rather than Central and Eastern, European political ideals.

East to Riga

But the course of Wagner's life had taken him eastwards to Königsberg and was soon to take him further north-east to Riga, a German city in Russian territory. In June 1837 Wagner was appointed musical director of the Riga theatre; he arrived there late in August. His invitation to Minna to join him, and her acceptance, suggests the recuperative powers of their marriage, and though the relationship continued turbulent for many years it also became increasingly stable amidst this turbulence.

The Wagners remained at Riga from autumn 1837 until summer 1839. In Wagner's career as a conductor, a notable point is marked by his performance of six of Beethoven's symphonies in the 1838-9 season. But conditions there offered little or no opportunity for performances either of the operas already composed by Wagner, or of that colossal opera on which he now embarked.

At Dresden in 1837, Wagner read the novel *Rienzi, the Last of the Tribunes* by the English writer and public figure Edward Bulwer (later known as Edward Bulwer-Lytton). Already, in Dresden, Wagner had sketched an opera on this subject, and in 1838 he completed his poetic treatment of the scenario and began musical composition. This was to take him over two years, in which he experienced the greatest deprivations and external turmoil of his life hitherto. His persistence with *Rienzi* foreshadows the tenacity with which he pursued operatic projects throughout his later life.

Rienzi is the story of a man who believes he has a mission vital for the dignity of his native state, a man whom that state at first welcomes and celebrates and subsequently rejects. It is not surprising that Wagner identified himself with such a figure; equally it is significant that Wagner felt driven to evoke, alongside an image of individual heroism, an image of the ideal republic, suffering from the oppressions of aristocrats who believe they were born to rule it, but deserving the liberation offered by the hero who knows that his gifts entitle him to lead it in the direction which only he can foresee.

The non-renewal of his contract by the Riga theatre in March 1839 may have been no great surprise. *Rienzi* and Riga clearly did not belong together, and it would have been sensible of Wagner, during the Riga period, to have imagined the possibility of performing the work in Paris. But Wagner's route to Paris, like so much of his life in the 1830s, was to be guided by chance and improvisation more than by any grand master-plan for his career.

Flight to Paris

By June 1839, he had a wife who may have been pregnant and creditors who were certainly pressing, but no passport with which to travel and thus escape the creditors and secure his wife's well-being. They borrowed from an old Königsberg friend a coach which took them as far as the Russian frontier, guarded by Cossack soldiers. While the watch was changing, they rushed over a ditch and out of range of the soldiers' guns. Avoiding Königsberg, they proceeded slowly over rough tracks in a cart; once it overturned, tossing them out and injuring Minna, who may well have miscarried at this point. Eventually reaching the port of Pillau (as it is now), they boarded a small ship before dawn, hiding below deck to evade the inspectors. The ship was bound for England. Driven by storms, it took refuge in a Norwegian fjord. Wagner later claimed that this experience had been the original occasion for his conception of his opera *Der Fliegende Holländer* (The Flying Dutchman) – though the earliest versions of the libretto set its action in Scotland.

In August the ship reached London, where Wagner attempted but failed to meet the author of *Rienzi*. Soon a boat was available for Boulogne, and the Wagners reached France on August 20th 1839. At Boulogne, by remarkable coincidence, Wagner met Meyerbeer, the leading composer of French opera, and at first Wagner's kindly friend and patron. Meyerbeer listened to Wagner's reading of the *Rienzi* libretto and offered him letters of introduction to the director of the Paris Opéra and to its leading conductor, Habeneck. Wagner reached Paris in mid-September.

But despite Meyerbeer's services Wagner's Paris years were to be the most impoverished, hard-working and unfulfilled of his whole career. And Wagner's sense of indignity was to lead him to make a scapegoat of Meyerbeer, and to some extent of the whole French musical and operatic tradition, despite the major debt which *Rienzi*, and all Wagner's operas of the 1840s, owe to that tradition.

One partial exception to Wagner's hostility towards French culture was furnished by his attitude to Berlioz. In November 1839 Wagner attended an early performance of Berlioz's *Romeo and Juliet* symphony, which immensely impressed him; and he retained sporadic contact with Berlioz throughout the 1840s and 1850s, up to the time when their respective operatic epics, Wagner's *Ring*, and Berlioz's *Trojans*, indicated unmistakably to both men the immense gap between their aims. The uniquely flexible combination of symphonic style, operatic writing and responsiveness to verbal imagery in Berlioz's *Romeo and Juliet* symphony is likely to have challenged Wagner. But Wagner's own later ideal of a *Gesamtkunstwerk*, a unity of all the arts under a single ideal, is diametrically opposed to the way in which textual, symphonic and balletic inspiration co-exist side by side in all Berlioz's musical works. An earlier work of Berlioz, his *Faust* settings, may have inspired Wagner to draft, in December 1839, the first movement of a *Faust* symphony, subsequently published by him as the *Faust* overture – the only one of Wagner's non-operatic overtures still to survive, however tenuously, in the concert repertoire.

In March 1840 the Théatre de la Renaissance accepted Wagner's *Das Liebesverbot* for performance, but almost immediately went bankrupt. In June 1840 the resourceful Wagner sent not *Rienzi*, but sketches of a new one-act opera to Meyerbeer, hoping that he would recommend the work to the Paris Opéra.

Leon Pillet, who was effectively the director of the Opéra, persuaded Wagner to sell the prose sketch, and Wagner's financial straits left him no choice but to accept. It was a sketch for *The Flying Dutchman*. Pillet passed it on to two other French librettists who, using it and much else as well, produced their own text for a French opera on the same theme, subsequently set by the composer Louis Dietsch. Meanwhile, Wagner set to work at once on the music of *The Flying Dutchman*, even before completing the composition of *Rienzi*.

Richard Wagner, drawn by Ernst Benedikt Kietz, another struggling artist in Paris between 1840 and 1842.

Creative but poor

The later months of 1840 were a high-water mark of Wagner's creativity in Paris, but marked also his most extreme financial predicament. In October and November he seems narrowly to have escaped imprisonment for his debts, and through these and later months he spent long periods of time copying scores by other composers and arranging and preparing vocal scores of operas.

He also earned a small trickle of money from musical journalism – an essay on German music was published in July 1840 and in that and the following year he favourably reviewed operas by leading French composers of the time, Meyerbeer, Auber and Halévy; it is significant that two of these three were Jews. Also in 1840 and 1841 Wagner composed three short novels, in one of which, entitled *A Pilgrimage to Beethoven*, the composer Beethoven is made to outline the possibility of a new synthesis of poetry and music involving continuous music – the synthesis which had already begun to prevail within German opera and which Wagner clearly saw himself commissioned to continue and fulfil.

By spring 1841 *The Flying Dutchman* scenario had been given its poetic treatment by Wagner; the musical composition was completed by November of the same year. Wagner's shorter compositions during the Paris period include a number of songs to French texts, and also a treatment of Heine's poem 'The Two Grenadiers', more famously set by Schumann. Wagner's treatment of the nostalgia of the Grenadiers for their dead emperor Napoleon displays enthusiastic identification with the image of the hero, and very little of the ironic qualifications placed on such identification by both Schumann and Heine. Wagner did meet Heine briefly during his Paris years, but another friendship was to prove more intellectually fruitful, that with the philologist Samuel Lehrs.

Lehrs led Wagner towards material on the legends which were to form the basis of his later operas of the 1840s, *Tannhäuser* and *Lohengrin*. The two men seem likely also to have discussed the intellectual revolutions in political and general philosophy associated with the figures of Feuerbach and Proudhon. Proudhon's slogan 'property is theft', and Feuerbach's powerful argument for seeing human views of God as projections of human deficiencies and social contradictions, played major parts in Wagner's social attitudes and in the foundations of his beliefs, as expressed both in his prose work and in his political activity of the late 1840s. A case could equally be made for seeing such ground-breaking critiques of existing political and religious institutions as embodied, though deviously and perhaps contra-dictorily, in the texts of *Tannhäuser* and *Lohengrin* themselves.

Wagner's resentment against Meyerbeer increased during 1841 and in early 1842, as the longed-for opportunities for performance of Wagner's operas in Paris failed to materialise. But *Rienzi*, a work based on the style of the most grand of French operas, was accepted in 1842 for performance in Dresden, and the Wagners seized the opportunity to leave Paris, in order to attend the Dresden première. As Wagner crossed from French- into German-speaking territory in 1842 he vowed 'eternal loyalty to my German fatherland'. There were also plans that year for a staging of *The Flying Dutchman* in Berlin; although these fell through, the work was to be performed in

The Dresden Opera House of the mid-nineteenth century, designed by Gottfried Semper, 1803-1837; in it *Rienzi, The Flying Dutchman* and *Tannhäuser* were first performed.

early January 1843, also in Dresden. By then Wagner had enjoyed his first major success, the premiere of Rienzi in Dresden, on October 20th 1842. The performers included Schröder-Devrient and, in the title role, the leading tenor Tichatschek. The triumph of Rienzi allowed the relative failure of *The Flying Dutchman* to pass without any great blow to Wagner's reputation.

Home to Dresden

After years of wandering, Wagner was back in what he increasingly regarded as his 'nation', his cultural homeland, and he remained based in Dresden for seven more years, during which, from 1843, he was employed as Kapellmeister in charge of all music performed in the court of the King of Saxony. His dependence on this court, and ultimately the king, indicated the limitations upon any possible conception of a German nation or an overall German culture. Nonetheless, the Dresden years allowed Wagner to form a basis, both mentally and in his way of life, for notions of how a general German artistic and intellectual culture could be deployed in the sphere of operatic music – notions which were to acquire a different shape in his mind after the political upheavals of 1849, and in the years of his own exile, but for which his stability and relative success in Dresden were clearly indispensable prerequisites.

In February 1843 Wagner published an autobiographical sketch in the magazine edited by Heinrich Laube. Already he had made prose sketches for his opera *Tannhäuser* while on holiday in Teplitz in Bohemia; the poem of *Tannhäuser* was completed in April 1843 and composition began in the summer of that year. In July 1843 he conducted male choral voices of over a thousand in *Das Liebesmahl der Apostel* (The Love Feast of the Apostles), in which the descent of the Holy Spirit on the apostles at Pentecost is given graphic form in Wagner's music. He is likely to have had in mind analogies between spiritual and artistic creative power such as those deployed two generations later by Mahler in the composition of his eighth symphony.

Wagner's intellectual ambitions were given a newly secure grounding in the apartment to which he moved in October 1843, where he was able to assemble, though at considerable expense, a library ranging widely in both contemporary and classical literature and featuring the tragedies of the Greek dramatists and the plays of Shakespeare, works to which he was to acknowledge his constant indebtedness. He also at this time pursued further his interests in the source material of Germanic epic – interests perhaps owed to some extent to Lehrs, but to which Wagner himself was to give influential shape and grandeur in his subsequent operas and music dramas.

In December 1844 the remains of the composer Weber were moved to Dresden, where they were dedicated in an inspiring ceremony involving a torch-lit procession with funeral music, composed by Wagner, followed the next morning at the graveside by an oration and a performance by a male chorus of a song. Wagner was orator, poet, composer and conductor.

A Berlin première
The Flying Dutchman was at last given its Berlin première in January 1844, and in the autumn of the same year Spontini, an Italian composer and a great master of French opera, was invited by Wagner to conduct his finest opera *La Vestale* (The Vestal Virgin). Wagner must have enjoyed the opportunity to patronise the French culture which had so signally rejected what he had to offer. In April 1845 the score of *Tannhäuser* was completed. In July Wagner went on holiday to Marienbad, where he immersed himself in studies of the legends concerning the figures of Lohengrin and Parzifal. At the same time he completed a very early prose draft for the opera which was subsequently to become *Die Meistersinger*, and in August a prose draft was completed for *Lohengrin*. Thus, to a significant extent, the entire shape of Wagner's later concerns with German history and mythology was present at this relatively early stage in his career. It is fascinating to speculate on the forms in which these concerns might have developed, had Wagner's career at Dresden continued uninterrupted.

Wagner's intellectual restlessness deployed itself equally in the practical matters concerned with his post. In 1846 he wrote an extended memorandum concerning the Royal orchestra, full of proposals for its re-organisation, the strengthening of all its component parts and the conditions of employment of its members. His proposals, rejected in 1847, were embodied in the orchestra he collected for his Festival Theatre at Bayreuth in 1876. Already in 1846 the success, despite opposition, of his conducting of Beethoven's 'Choral' Symphony on Palm Sunday indicated the extent to which his gifts involved a re-thinking of attitudes to performance as much as to composition. He was committed to a view of the conductor's function as involving creative and revelatory interpretation of music, rather than mere co-ordination of its performers. Separate thematic groups were,

Rosalie Marbach, née Wagner, 1803-1837; an elder sister of the composer, a successful actress in Dresden, Prague and Leipzig.

under his baton, sharply differentiated in tempo and dynamics – as if they embodied distinct dramatic characters. Such an approach required detailed and extensive rehearsal; ensemble playing could be ragged when this was not available.

Drafts of *Lohengrin* were completed in 1846 and 1847 and the score was finished by the end of April 1848. In these years Wagner was conducting an intensive reading of Greek authors in translation, including the Oresteian trilogy by Aeschylus, which has been seen as an intellectual parallel to Wagner's own cycle *The Ring of the Nibelungs*, and also the comic plays of the Greek poet–dramatist Aristophanes, notable for satiric criticism of Athenian contemporaries. In Wagner's operas of the 1840s, and in the *Ring* itself, satire seems relatively muted alongside celebration, tragedy and mythic enactment. Yet the tone of criticism is never entirely absent and should perhaps be given a larger place than is customary in our picture of Wagner during these years.

Wagner was also involved in the revision of one of the masterpieces of the eighteenth century – a reform opera of its own time, the *Iphigénie en Aulide* of Gluck, which he conducted in his own version in February 1847. In October 1847 *Rienzi* was premièred in Berlin; its images of large-scale political upheaval were to be mirrored on a German, and indeed European, scale in political events from spring 1848 onwards. These events were to involve Wagner directly in 1849 and to lead to the precipitate end of his years in Dresden. These years had been stable and financially secure by his standards (though not by most others) and had seen the creation of a body of work stylistically coherent, dramatically powerful and increasingly individual. Major features of the 1840s achievement were to permeate all Wagner's subsequent masterpieces.

Chapter 3

The Operas: 1835-1848

Das Liebesverbot: *Plot*

Friedrich is a German regent ruling the island of Sicily in the absence of its king. He passes a law against all sexual activity, and even those emotions of love associated with it, except within the marriage bond; those who break the law will die. Claudio, a young nobleman, is condemned under the law. His sister Isabella, a novice nun, is persuaded by their friend Lucio to appeal to Friedrich. Friedrich had once been married to Mariana, a fellow novice of Isabella, but had rejected her for the sake of his own political ambition. He now hypocritically, and against the letter of his own law, offers Claudio freedom if Isabella will sleep with him. Isabella, pretending to agree, sends Mariana to their rendezvous, which is a carnival in fancy dress. In this ceremony (itself forbidden by the new laws) Friedrich's true character is exposed. He offers himself up to his own penalty of death. The people set his laws aside, and set him free; their own king returns to inaugurate a new period of sensual love and emotional freedom.

Das Liebesverbot: *Commentary*

The setting is in Sicily in a medieval period in which Wagner could have found the name of Friedrich associated with a Holy Roman Emperor, Friedrich II. The names of most of the characters and the outline of the plot are taken from Shakespeare's *Measure for Measure*, whose setting is not Sicily but Vienna. A Viennese setting for the opera might have aroused censorship; but a Sicilian setting was not innocuous, given the crushingly reactionary rule of Naples and Sicily by the restored Bourbon kings in the 1830s.

Changes from Shakespeare's plot are caused by Wagner's omission of the character of the Duke. He, in Shakespeare, arranges a moderately happy ending, with marriages acknowledged and death sentences avoided, and also becomes a participant in the comic and near-tragic confusions of the action, eventually himself asking for the hand of Isabella in marriage. In Wagner, Isabella presides over the circumvention of Friedrich's law and the exposure of his character, and is eventually married to Lucio, whose character is endorsed by Wagner far more than by Shakespeare. The tone of Wagner's adaptation of *Measure for Measure* is unique amongst all interpretations of this puzzling play; and the absence of supernatural elements in the opera is unusual in Wagner's works. Love – forbidden by Friedrich, praised by the other characters and finally inaugurated as a new social principle of the kingdom – is undisguisedly sensual. Thus the work openly appeals to the ideal of glorified humanity as true divinity, an ideal acknowledged by Wagner in his prose writings, and significant, but scarcely so directly acknowledged, elsewhere in his operas.

The musical language echoes contemporary Italian operas, particularly those of Rossini and Bellini, whom Wagner greatly admired, in its melodic fluency and the relatively light orchestral scoring. There are proportionally more ensembles than in *Die Feen* or *Rienzi*. Particularly successful is the duet for Isabella and her brother Claudio, in which he gradually realises all that he will lose by accepting a heroic martyr's death. Friedrich has a powerful, though more traditionally Germanic, solo in the second act, in which he battles between his puritanism, his lust and his duties to the law. The two finales and the opening sequence of Act One are well organised in their musical continuity, and again full of melodic interest. There are several recurring musical themes; one, associated with the prohibition against love, is used to indicate the relation between the repression of love and its subconscious presence in the minds of Friedrich and others.

The social context of the action is largely aristocratic; but a police chief, an innkeeper and servants give the work a social breadth scarcely found elsewhere in Wagner's works. The replacement of the regent by the returning king corresponds to the belief expressed elsewhere by Wagner that democracy, while compatible with allegiance to a monarch, could scarcely survive the rule of the traditional aristocracy. In this and other ways *Das Liebesverbot* stands out as the most straightforwardly revolutionary of Wagner's works and as one whose specific virtues were scarcely reincarnated anywhere in his later productions.

Rienzi: *Plot*

The setting is Rome just before the middle of the fourteenth century. Rienzi is a lawyer in the service of the Pope. As the action starts, his sister, Irene, is about to be abducted by the nobleman, Paolo Orsini, and his followers. A rival family, the

Colonnas, challenge them; Adriano Colonna, who loves Irene, protects her. The fighting is halted by the arrival of Rienzi. The people urge him to take over rule in the city and restore order. Rienzi's brother was murdered by a Colonna, but Adriano promises him his support; Rienzi foregoes vengeance and entrusts his sister to Adriano. Refusing the title of king he accepts that of Tribune of the People.

In the immense second act young noblemen celebrate the glory of Rienzi's regime and the success of their mission of peace throughout Italy, while the noble families resentfully submerge former mutual rivalries in conspiracy against Rienzi. Rienzi, receiving ambassadors from foreign powers, demands that the people of Rome enjoy their former right of election to the Holy Roman Emperorship. In a ballet the theme of Rienzi's Rome as a reincarnation of ancient Rome is celebrated. Orsini stabs Rienzi; his breastplate saves him. Colonna's men have tried to seize the Capitol. The people and the other senators demand that the traitors die, but Adriano and Irene succeed in persuading Rienzi to pardon them.

In Act Three Rienzi has been forced to lead a people's army against the rebellious nobles: Adriano faces the choice of betraying Rienzi, the brother of his lover, or of fighting against his own father. Rienzi refuses Adriano's request to intercede between the sides and eventually returns in triumph, having killed Orsini and Colonna. Adriano, in despair, vows vengeance for his father.

In the fourth act discontent has mounted against the regime, fostered by protests from the Pope and resentment from the Germans, angry at Rienzi's interference with their own rights of imperial election. It is claimed that Rienzi seeks not the suppression of the nobles, but personal alliance with them, as witness the bond between Irene and Adriano. Adriano emerges openly as an enemy of Rienzi and urges the crowd to revenge. The Pope excommunicates Rienzi and his followers desert him. Irene, still loyal to her brother, is rejected by Adriano.

In the fifth act Rienzi voices a prayer for strength and preservation. His sister vows her abiding loyalty. He urges her to leave him and join Adriano. The people throw stones at Rienzi and set the Capitol on fire. Rienzi speaks proudly of his future fame and dies in Irene's arms. Adriano seeks to rescue her, but the building collapses and buries him with Irene and Rienzi.

Rienzi: *Commentary*

At its full length *Rienzi* is perhaps Wagner's longest opera, and certainly his most magniloquent. As against the novel which was Wagner's source, Rienzi is unmarried, and thus more proudly isolated. In the novel he is deserted by the people; in Wagner's libretto he is betrayed by the nobles, the papacy and foreign powers, and also by Adriano. Yet Wagner's hero is scarcely more sympathetic through such isolation, unless in his finely melodic prayer in the last act. Earlier scenes of popular rising and rejoicing, as at the end of Act One, evoke some energetic and exciting music, with very demanding chorus writing. Much of Act Two is given over to ballet music of relentless major keys and repetitive rhythms.

The narrative exhibits certain parallels with that of Mozart's late opera *La Clemenza di Tito* (The Clemency of Titus) in which, as in *Rienzi*, nobles conspire against a benign rule, a conflagration threatens the city, and a sense of duty and civic ceremony tend to dwarf or exhaust any sense of powerful individuality in the work's hero. But there would be grounds for seeing Rienzi as a man not subdued, but corrupted, by power and by the single-mindedness which it forces upon him; while Adriano, a double traitor, stands out as more sympathetic and understandable. (The role is assigned to a mezzo-soprano voice, a remarkable echo of both the Mozart opera and eighteenth-century tradition in general).

Remarks by Wagner in 'On State and Religion', an essay of the mid-1860s, illuminate some features of *Rienzi*. Wagner suggests the necessity of a ruler's sacrificing a certain degree of egoism, on behalf of the stability of his state, and indicates how a people can be persuaded to serve group interests by rhetoric suggesting that their own interests are at stake. In this essay Wagner also perceives, much in the spirit of Machiavelli's *Discourses*, that the success, in any one state, of patriotic propaganda, generates violence towards other states. *Rienzi*, like *Das Liebesverbot*, is a work from which any genuinely supernatural force, as distinct from state religion, is absent; in the essay Wagner argues that religion, if taken seriously, will lead a ruler away from political reason towards preoccupation with other worlds.

Rienzi is Wagner's most purely political work and in some ways, despite its grandiose ceremony, his most depressing. It was revived in Berlin and Frankfurt in 1933, the year of Hitler's accession to power, and Hitler had already written, of his attendance at a performance of the work around 1906, 'In that hour it all began'.

Der fliegende Holländer: *Plot*

A ship casts anchor in a fjord on the Norwegian coast. It is the ship of Daland. He and his crew go on shore leaving a steersman on watch. The storm which has driven him to land subsides; the

Senta's leap of faith, from *The Flying Dutchman*.

steersman dozes. As the storm blows up again another ship comes into view. Its sails are red; it is the ship of the Flying Dutchman. The Dutchman is allowed to land once in every seven years, seeking redemption from the curse of immortality under which he suffers. Daland approaches the Dutchman, who offers him riches in exchange for a night's hospitality. Daland, delighted by this, is equally delighted by the Dutchman's interest in his daughter Senta.

The scene changes to Daland's house. Women are spinning while their lovers are away at sea. Senta gazes at a picture on the wall, which shows a pale man with a dark beard in dark costume. She sings the ballad of the Flying Dutchman, whose curse was laid on him in response to a blasphemous oath. She offers herself as the salvation for the unknown seaman. Her lover Erik is horrified. He tells her of his dream, in which her father had brought home a stranger similar to the seafarer in the portrait. He leaves in despair. As Senta gazes again on the picture her father appears, and the Dutchman with him. Recognising in him the subject of Erik's dream and the portrait, she tells him of her longing to redeem him. He warns her that if she were unfaithful she would die. She promises faithfulness. Daland suggests that they be betrothed.

The scene changes back to the seacoast, a bay with a rocky shore. The Norwegian sailors are feasting and drinking on deck; women join them, and they all call out to the crew of the Dutchman's ship. At first they are silent but, as the appeals become more frenetic, a storm rises, and the Dutch crew bursts into ghostly song, terrifying the Norwegian sailors. Senta is reminded by Erik of her former pledges to him. The Dutchman, overhearing this, is angered, but offers to release Senta from her vow, telling her that he is saving Senta from his own fate. He boards his ship. Senta, proclaiming her eternal faithfulness, casts herself into the waters. The Dutchman's ship and its crew sink. The Dutchman and Senta are revealed in the skies, locked in eternal embrace.

Der fliegende Holländer: *Commentary*

Wagner's original conception took the form of a single act, as he supposed this would enable a Parisian performance to be achieved more readily. When his hopes of a Paris première were abandoned, he recast it in three acts. Cosima Wagner's 1901 Bayreuth production restored the one-act form. The work's musical continuity may be seen in the key of D, with which it begins and ends, and in the powerful recurrences of themes, and repeated intervals, within music associated with the Dutchman's suffering and with Senta's ballad. Wagner later claimed, with some exaggeration, that the music of Senta's ballad lay at the root of the whole work. Certainly connections can be traced between it and the Dutchman's monologue, Erik's dream-narration, the duet between Senta and the Dutchman and the finale of the whole work.

Some ensembles are prominent; duets, for example, between the Dutchman and Daland, and the Dutchman and Senta. But it is noteworthy that Senta and her lover Erik scarcely ever sing in duet. Choruses are prominent at the beginning of each of the three sections, and the first scene of the third section, organised as an opposition of two choruses, is one of the most immediately dramatic (rather than merely ceremonial) choral scenes in all Wagner's work. Many of the musical numbers display an expansive articulation of melody, in four- and eight-bar phrases, more prevalent in *Tannhäuser* and still more in *Lohengrin*: but the setting of Erik's dream is remarkable for the close fit between the rhythms of the music and of the words, and thus for the admirably unpredictable and asymmetrical nature of the rhythm.

Of all Wagner's operas *The Flying Dutchman* most obviously displays his debt to the late work of Beethoven, particularly the first movement of the 'Choral' Symphony, with which it shares the key of D Minor and an atmosphere of brooding intensity and sudden outbursts of furious energy. In acknowledging and emulating such an influence, Wagner was unusual in the early 1840s. Echoes of Mendelssohn's storm music, and parallels with

Rosina Raisbeck as Senta, Josef Metternich as The Dutchman; Covent Garden 1950/1951.

the high emotional rhetoric of Weber's heroes, are less surprising.

The Dutchman is the first of many Wagner heroes to be dominated by a need for redemption and, to a lesser extent, a consciousness of guilt. Senta is the purest case of the Wagner heroine who offers to redeem the guilt and suffering of the man she loves. The structure leaves little doubt in an audience's mind that the Dutchman will eventually be redeemed from the terms of his curse. The action is thus associated with the process, rather than the fact, of redemption, and in particular with the tension between Senta's repeated claims of fidelity and the uncertainty, amounting to scepticism, which evokes these claims. The Dutchman's eventual redemption, indeed, is provoked as much by his scepticism, aroused by Senta's involvement with Erik, as by his belief in her. Thus the desire for certainty, and a belief in betrayal, join hand in hand to produce the work's denouement.

The other characters in the opera, even including the small roles of the steersman and Mary, Senta's nurse, are realised concisely but credibly. Modern productions have found it possible, and even effective, to imagine the action of the work as framed by the consciousness, the imagination or the dreams of one or more of these other characters.

Tannhäuser: *Plot*

The first act begins on the Venusberg, a mountainous scene centred on the goddess Venus, who, surrounded by sirens and nymphs, presides over their dances and celebrations. Her human lover, Tannhäuser, rests his head in her lap, but he has had more than enough of Venus's immortal charms and pleasures. He sings her praises but begs her for release. Angered, she eventually yields as he names the Virgin Mary. Venus and her domain vanish, and Tannhäuser finds himself in a sunlit valley. Pilgrims pass, followed by the Landgrave of Thuringia, who presides over a court of minstrel knights. They recognise and greet Tannhäuser and beg him to stay with them. One of them, Wolfram, speaks to him of the pleasure which his return to their court will give to the Landgrave's daughter, Elizabeth. Tannhäuser, longing to see her again, joins them.

Act Two is set in the 'Hall of song' in the Landgrave's castle, the Wartburg. Elizabeth, who has abandoned the hall while Tannhäuser has been away, returns joyfully to it and is reunited with Tannhäuser. They sing of their love. Guests arrive from neighbouring kingdoms. The Landgrave praises the art of music and calls on the minstrels to sing the praises of love: Elizabeth will reward the most successful with a prize. Each in turn sings of the ideal purity of love, and its immunity from the demands of the senses. Tannhäuser scornfully rejects such conceptions. One of the knights, Biterolf, challenges Tannhäuser to a duel. Tannhäuser, scorning him, bursts angrily and triumphantly into the song with which he had praised Venus in the first act. The guests are appalled, the women leave, the knights threaten Tannhäuser. Elizabeth begs for mercy. The remorseful Tannhäuser accepts the Landgrave's demand that he join the pilgrims on their way to Rome and beg the Pope for pardon.

Elizabeth, in Act Three, prays for the long absent Tannhäuser. Wolfram sings with melancholy of his own frustrated love for Elizabeth. Tannhäuser at last returns and tells Wolfram, in an extended narration, of his expectant and joyful arrival in Rome and of the majesty of the church's ceremonial. He moves on to describe the anger of the Pope at his sin and the papal condemnation under which has been laid: only when the Pope's staff shoots forth green leaves, he has been told, can he be forgiven. In despair he tells Wolfram that he will return to the Venusberg. Venus is heard summoning him. Wolfram urges Tannhäuser to

Tannhäuser outrages the Landgrave and the minstrel-knights and blights Elizabeth's hopes; the Wartburg scene, *Tannhäuser*, in a print of 1845.

remember his love for Elizabeth and finally enunciates her name. At this moment an off-stage chorus proclaims her death; Venus, overcome, disappears. As Elizabeth's body is carried on in funeral procession Tannhäuser calls upon her, as a saint, to pray for him. He dies as pilgrims enter telling of a miracle – the Pope's staff has burst into leaf.

Tannhäuser: *Commentary*

Wagner made revisions to *Tannhäuser* at a number of stages in his life. The most thoroughgoing of these were called forth by the prospect of performance in Paris in 1861. Though the performances were unsuccessful, for reasons largely out of Wagner's control, he incorporated a number of them (including the greatly extended music associated with Venus in Act One) in the final version to which he set his hand in 1875. Changes at an earlier stage, in the later 1840s, include the final appearances of Venus, and of the knights with the body of Elizabeth. Wieland Wagner's Bayreuth production of 1954 offered an effective synthesis of all the various versions.

Superficially the theme of the opera is the contest between sensual and spiritual love in Tannhäuser. But, as elsewhere, Wagner has given an apparently combative and religious appearance to a work whose ultimate conception was psychological and critical. In an essay of 1852, 'On the Performing of *Tannhäuser*' Wagner wrote 'Tannhäuser is always fully and to the utmost', and described his 'unending need to adjust the communication of his instinctive feelings to the over-riding demands of custom'. Tannhäuser would thus be characterised not significantly by love for Venus, but rather by a rejection of the repetitive nature of both her demands and those of German feudal and artistic custom to which he finds himself increasingly subjected in the contest of the second act. At no point in the work is he shown as rejecting the love of Elizabeth, nor as contrasting it with his service to Venus.

A climax of Tannhäuser's critical resentment against conventional society is reached when his third-act narration passes from the glories of the journey to Rome into an evocation of the stern inhumanity of the Roman Pope. Tannhäuser, like Wagner, can find no adequate resolution for this resentment. His final appeal to Venus is despairing and self-contradictory; his redemption by the prayers and the name of Elizabeth comes too late to allow him to envisage any home for his love within human social forms. This tension, between love and social institutions, is presented with more sustained power, but less critical force, in *Tristan und Isolde* twelve years later. *Lohengrin* similarly revolves on the incompatibility between the energies (shown there as supernatural) available to the confident trusting lover and the demands of combative human social relationships. The resolution of *Tannhäuser* is multiply melodramatic, with events crowding into the work's last few moments, whereas that of *Lohengrin* proceeds slowly but steadily towards genuine tragedy.

But other features of *Tannhäuser* have made it probably the more popular of the two works. Though there is little continuity between its scenes and musical numbers, several of these numbers have successfully established themselves in the concert repertoire, particularly Elizabeth's greeting to the hall of song at the start of Act Two and Wolfram's evocation of the evening star in Act Three. The entry of the guests in Act Two, like the bridal procession in the third act of *Lohengrin*, is well known as a separate orchestral piece. Tannhäuser's invocation of Venus necessarily functions as a recurring theme, and a repeated musical cadence, known (independently of Wagner) as the 'Dresden Amen' is used to evoke the Roman church and its claims to spiritual purity.

The work sets the keys of E major and E flat major against one another; their opposition evokes that between Venus and spiritual love. In Tannhäuser's Act Three narration his audience with the Pope is presented in the key of E flat, which yields to the return of the E major key associated with the Venusberg. A final return to E flat indicates the salvation of Tannhäuser's soul. The song contest calls forth conservative and square rhythms and melodic structures, lending force to Tannhäuser's outbursts. But his own song in honour of the goddess is in many ways as

Autographed page
from the first act of
Wagner's *Tannhäuser*.

rhythmically predictable as that of his rivals. The music of Venus
herself is more subtly adapted to the demands of the words. The
most rhythmically flexible, and least conventionally operatic,
passage in the score is Tannhäuser's Act Three narration: in this
the oscillations of his desires are replaced by a bitter, but
coherent, reflection on the necessary contrast between his warm
emotional energies and the cold dryness of the world in which
he moves.

Lohengrin: *Plot*

The opera is set early in the tenth century AD in the city of
Antwerp. In the first act King Henry meets the nobles of Brabant
and encourages them to help defend Germany against the
invading pagan Hungarians in the East. Having secured their
agreement, he tries to resolve a dispute amongst the nobles,
explained by Count Friedrich von Telramund. The Dukedom of
Brabant is vacant; the old Duke had entrusted to Friedrich the
guardianship of his children, Gottfried and Elsa. Elsa, he states,
had made away with the boy Gottfried. Friedrich has foregone
his right to marry Elsa, taking instead Ortrud as his wife. He
charges Elsa with treachery and sorcery. If his charges are
proven he himself will accede to the Dukedom of Brabant. The
king summons Elsa, who refuses to answer Friedrich's charges
and tells of a dream vision in which a knightly champion of her
cause appeared to her. The king sets up a trial by combat and
Friedrich takes his stand against whatever champion may appear
to defend Elsa; after long suspense a strange knight is seen

approaching, in a boat on the river, drawn by a swan. He steps to the shore, greets King Henry and announces himself as Elsa's champion. She rapturously accepts his protection. He at once explains that she must not ask him his name or his origin. She accepts these conditions; the knight defies Friedrich, the king appeals to God to overrule the result of the combat and Lohengrin (for it is he) and Friedrich draw their swords. The fight is brief. Lohengrin is victorious; Friedrich is shamed, but his life is spared.

The first scene of the second act takes place within the fortress at Antwerp. Friedrich complains to Ortrud of the disgrace that has fallen on him for making the challenge she urged on him. Ortrud scornfully upbraids his cowardly defeatism, and claims that the mysterious knight's power would end if Elsa were ask him his name. Ortrud, under a guise of humility, appeals to Elsa, who is preparing for her wedding, and arouses her sense of generosity and sympathy. In the second scene of the act, the herald announces Friedrich's banishment and proclaims that the strange knight will take the title not of Duke, but of Protector of Brabant. A wedding procession emerges and is interrupted, first by Ortrud and then by Friedrich. Friedrich accuses the knight of sorcery and demands that he reveal his name to all the people. The knight replies that only Elsa can elicit such a revelation from him. He discovers that she is disturbed by his silence. As the bridal couple reach the top step of the church, Ortrud casts up her arm in a gesture of triumph against them.

The third act opens with the bridal march. When the lovers are left alone, their talk moves from their love to the knight's reassurances, in the face of Elsa's mounting uncertainty of her own worthiness, and her increasing anxiety as to his nature and origins. Ultimately, her questioning will no longer be silenced; she asks him his name. At this point Friedrich, with knights, bursts into the chamber. Lohengrin kills Friedrich and orders the knights to bear away his body; he will give the account of himself which he owes to the king and the whole people.

In the second scene of the act, on the banks of the river Scheldt, the body of Friedrich is brought in. Elsa enters, Lohengrin follows her and explains to the king that he can no longer lead the nobles of Brabant into battle, that his powers are no longer available for knightly service and that Elsa has broken her vow. He is a knight of the Grail, the son of Parzival; his name is Lohengrin. Such knights are given supreme power, but must remain unknown while on earth. The swan which drew Lohengrin's boat reappears, and he explains that if he and Elsa had lived in marriage for a year, her brother Gottfried would have been restored to her. He gives Elsa his sword, his horn and his ring, all to be given to Gottfried should he ever return. As Lohengrin prepares to leave in the swan boat, Ortrud defiantly claims that the swan is Gottfried, transformed by her sorcery. Lohengrin prays, a dove descends and hovers over the boat, Lohengrin looses the chain around the swan, the swan vanishes and in its place Gottfried steps forth. Lohengrin proclaims him as the Duke of Brabant. Ortrud and then Elsa fall to the ground and Lohengrin vanishes from sight amidst general mourning.

Lohengrin: *Commentary*

The swan in the Age of Industry; beneath the stage at the Paris Opèra during *Lohengrin* (a print of 1892).

Wagner drew together material from three epics of the twelfth and thirteenth centuries, one of them (anonymous) entitled *Lohengrin*, the others, including *Parzival*, by the great German poet Wolfram von Eschenbach, later the source of Wagner's last opera. Wagner himself was responsible for the historical detail which gives to the opera's action a remarkably plausible flavour of the Holy Roman Empire in its early Germanic period.

On the face of it the chief conflict is between the Christian knightly characters of the king and Lohengrin (with Elsa), and the pagan Ortrud with her husband Friedrich. But Wagner plausibly explained in his 1851 essay 'A Communication to my Friends' that it was not the 'leanings towards Christian supernaturalism' that he had wished the story to expound. Indeed, the dramatic theme of *Lohengrin* remains for the greater part of the opera as elusive as the identity of its hero.

We encounter a sequence of possible themes; first the combination of feudal aristocrats under a monarchic overlord against pagan invaders; immediately following this, aristocratic dynastic quarrels, and the intervention of supernatural power to resolve them. Two forces for unity emerge in the first act, Henry, as king, and the divinity which Lohengrin brings to earth and represents. The opposition of Ortrud and Friedrich to Lohengrin can equally be construed as an opposition to Henry's imperial power. But their energies are deployed, during the second and third acts, within the precarious balance of the relationship between Lohengrin and Elsa.

Thus the issue comes to be the relation between trust and scepticism, love and individual uncertainty. Ortrud and Friedrich represent a model of human relationships based on the perpetual necessity of challenge and response. Lohengrin cannot refuse Elsa's challenge, nor can she, as an independent human being, withhold that challenge. While the opera offers a possible model, of identity submerged or within the loyalty owed to a social or supernatural unifying force, a different model triumphs at the end of the opera; the model of identity defined by, and endlessly disposed to, struggle and contestation.

For Lohengrin's identity to be fixed is a mark of failure; whereas the sword, the horn and the ring which he leaves behind are tokens of identity which function only in the absence of their owner. Similarly, he has refused a defined social position as Duke of Brabant. At his departure the dukedom is again occupied by Gottfried, but the path to the supernatural is closed off, and we are left with a specifically human, and endangered, kingdom. Yet the music of the opera glorifies the supernatural aura of Lohengrin in a way that leaves the issue between these models of identity superbly unresolved. In many ways *Lohengrin* anticipates all the concerns of the *Ring* cycle, in its preoccupation with the dangerous necessities, and the necessary dangers, of signification, identity and decipherability of signs.

There are few separate musical numbers in *Lohengrin*, though they include some of the finest and most memorable melodic writing of the score: King Henry's prayer and Elsa's dream vision in the first act, and Lohengrin's narration in Act Three. There are virtually no duets with characters singing in harmony with one another – only brief passages between Elsa and Ortrud in the first scene of Act Two and between Elsa and Lohengrin in the first scene of Act Three.

The majority of the opera is given over to dialogue, in which individual characters announce their positions, stake their claims and define their conflicts with one another at considerable but largely symmetrical length. Such dialogue takes place in a fascinatingly poised balance between free recitative and remarkably regular four-bar and eight-bar rhythmic phrases, whose symmetry is enhanced by the pervasive 4/4 time-signature which prevails throughout virtually the whole opera. The work also contains a number of powerful ensembles in which solo characters join with the chorus; for example in the sequence after the King's prayer in Act One, and above all at the climactic confrontation between the characters at the interruption of the bridal procession in Act Two. There are also crucial choruses without solo singers, punctuated only by announcements of the herald; through these choruses musical reality is given to the gathered feudal aristocracy which is so essential a datum of the opera's historical action. Such choruses appear at the centre of the second act and thus of the whole work, at the start of the opera's final scene and (the finest of all) at the arrival of Lohengrin in Act One.

Despite the regular 4/4 time-signatures, Wagner brilliantly avoids repetition or monotony by a close observation of the rhythms of natural verbal declamation. In this respect *Lohengrin* points the way to the theories of music's adaptation to verbal demands which Wagner was to elaborate in his prose writings of the next few years.

But the score is unified in broad ways by the operation of certain key relationships. The work begins and ends in A major, a key frequently associated with the supernatural origins of Lohengrin. Lohengrin's encounter with Elsa in Act One oscillates between A and A flat major and minor, and there is a certain amount of association of A flat major with the character of Elsa; thus, as in *Tannhäuser*, the interval of a semitone indicates at once the closeness to, and the distance from, one another of central characters and ideas. One might see this interval as registering a poise between collective trust and individual sceptical energy, at the heart of the drama's emotional meaning. The key of F sharp minor (relative minor of A major) is associated with Ortrud and her husband Friedrich, and the key of C is associated with the king and the knights. Thus, the central key of A is surrounded by two lesser centres equidistant from it.

The most advanced harmonic writing of the score occurs in the first scene of the second act, where the tension between

Ortrud and her husband is reflected in constant, and often explosive, changes of key: thus the model of relationships dominated by challenge is given an harmonic instantiation.

Two recurrent themes stand out from the flow of non-repetitive music. The theme associated with the Grail begins the whole work: soon after Lohengrin's arrival in the first act, the theme associated with the notion of a forbidden question takes its place beside it. This theme resounds with powerful prophetic effect at the end of the second act. The revelation of Lohengrin's identity in his narration in Act Three brings with it a recurrence of the opening music of the opera's prelude. This prelude is itself not only an intensely beautiful piece of orchestral writing, but in many ways encapsulates a certain view of the drama; it embodies the image of a heavenly being descending to earth and returning again to the place from which he came.

Chapter 4

Exile and Lover

1848 has become known to historians of Europe as the year of revolutions. For Wagner it was his thirty-fifth year, and halfway through his allotted biblical span of seventy years, which was indeed to prove his actual life span. For fifteen years he had pursued, to a point of recognised success, his chosen mission as a composer of dramatic music. His apparent failure, up to the end of the Paris years, is likely to have filled him, not only with hostility towards the musical establishments of his time, but also, however much he may have suppressed this, with a sense of shame at his own failure, and at the price this was exacting from himself and from his wife. From 1842 onwards his life may be felt to have acquired a growing sense of stability, as his shame passed over, first into an increasingly triumphant self-confidence, and later into a deployment of that confidence in musical and social criticism of his world.

Tannhäuser and *Lohengrin* were operas whose dramatic ambition and physical scale marked a turning point for Wagner's whole career. (The three-act shape familiar in Wagner's subsequent operas is only firmly established in his work from *Tannhäuser* onwards.) Their subject matter and dramatic treatment show Wagnerian self-confidence turning into Wagnerian social criticism. Tannhäuser's oscillation between Venus and Elizabeth results from a consistent pursuit of love; his outburst in the second act of the opera is directed against the inadequate perceptions of, and commitments to, human love implied in the songs of his fellow minstrels. It is their inadequate sexual energy, just as in the third act it is the hypocrisy of the papal condemnation, which drive Tannhäuser, despite himself, back into the arms of Venus. Institutions of aristocratic courtesy and papal theocracy stand condemned by the desires of a tortured, but self-liberating, hero.

In *Lohengrin*, again, an ostensible conflict between paganism and Christianity only partially conceals a drama concerned with competing projects for social regeneration, on a basis of a restoration of energies hitherto trammelled by the aristocratic

Barricades in the Dresden streets in 1849.

feudal forms, which the first act so monumentally deploys. Lohengrin's project founders on Elsa's unwillingness to take him at face value. She insists on asking questions. What is true for Elsa is by extension true for her whole society. New energies are needed and they can be supplied only by outsiders; what is in question is not the availability of outsiders but the willingness of the societies to submit to them on their own terms.

The dramatic structure of *Lohengrin* thus notably echoes that of *Rienzi*, conceived ten years earlier. But what *Rienzi* presents as the pathetic melodrama of a misunderstood hero, *Lohengrin* presents as the necessary collision of competing social visionaries, coupled with the inevitable self-preservation of self-frustrated societies. The next eighteen months in the 'real' world of central European politics and in Wagner's own life and career were to prove how uncannily prophetic his works had been.

Year of revolutions

1848, the year of revolutions, was heralded by unrest in Sicily and Italy, but the most momentous outbreak of social discontent came in the Vienna rising of March, which Wagner greeted with

a signed poem entitled 'Greetings from Saxony to the Viennese'.
In April he completed the scoring of *Lohengrin*; in May he
submitted to the Saxon court a document entitled 'Plan for the
Organisation of a German National Theatre for the Kingdom of
Saxony,' in which he argued for the maintenance of a permanent
drama school, for regular training for members of the operatic
chorus and above all for the setting up of a self-managing
association involving dramatists and composers. It is notable,
throughout this and the next year, how far Wagner's abilities,
improvisational and suited to the needs of the time, emerged in
the form of prose and occasionally poetic writings rather than of
musical composition.

One of the most momentous, and with hindsight the most
unusual, of his writings appeared in June, the publication of an
address delivered under the title 'How do Republican
Endeavours Stand in Relation to the Monarchy?' In this address
Wagner condemned the failings of the unreconstructed
aristocracy of his time, while arguing for the possibility, and
indeed desirability, of retaining a monarchy, and, rather incon-
gruously, urging the setting up of a people's militia. This

combination of Machiavellian and anti-Machiavellian republican arguments is given a millenarian thrust by a polemic against money and a money-based economy, perhaps the dominant note in the address. It is tempting to see here a reflection of Wagner's own chronic cash crisis, but his years in employment in Dresden had, without removing the crisis, to some extent lessened its pressure on him.

It is more relevant to trace Wagner's arguments to his contact with revolutionary circles in German thought; for example, his friendship with August Röckel, his assistant conductor at Dresden, who was the editor of the *Volksblätter*, a radical popular journal. In 1849 Röckel introduced Wagner to the Russian anarchist Bakunin, who in his turn knew Marx and Engels. Bakunin has been seen with some plausibility as one model for the figure of Siegfried in Wagner's *Ring*; and the years immediately after 1848, crucial for the development of Wagner's dramatic plans for the *Ring* cycle, were also the years in which Marx's social and economic thought, driven by the possibilities and the eventual failures of European revolution, were to assume their most incisively analytic and prophetic forms.

In 1848 Wagner was putting in a great deal of reading on texts which he was later to use as the sources for his drama of the Nibelungs. These texts took him back, from the heroic early medieval narrative of the *Nibelungenlied*, to more remote Nordic and Teutonic sources implying, and to some extent themselves setting forth, an entire history of the gods, their generation, their interrelations and their dealings with humanity.

Thus Wagner's commitment to ideals of human heroism was taking the shape of an involvement with historiography and theology. It is no accident that the planning for a Nibelung drama went side by side with projects for a drama whose hero would be Jesus of Nazareth, with other plans concerning Friedrich Barbarossa (a medieval ruler of the Holy Roman Empire, around whom legends had long since clustered) and also with projects for a work based on the hero of Homer's *Iliad*, Achilles. In all of these dramatic projects, the notion of a humanity which at its highest level is divine, and which can thus justifiably cast off the shackles of supposed divine tutelage, and vindicate itself as the model for a new human society, stands out with increasing clarity.

An essay published in the *Volksblätter* of April 1849 under the title 'The Revolution' contains the phrase 'only the free man is holy'. It is not entirely clear if the essay is by Wagner: it would be true to the spirit of Wagner's subsequent music dramas to reverse the emphasis – only the holy man is free. A further phrase in the essay indicates the relevance of such ideals to a more immediately material revolutionary dynamic: 'Since all are equal I shall destroy all dominion of one over the other.' Wagner seems at this time to be involved in planning the manufacture of hand grenades and in the organisation of explosive material. Explosives need a target and, as European events had developed, it seemed likely that the target for Wagnerian explosives would be the breasts of his fellow Germans.

Earlier in 1849 the King of Prussia, Friedrich Wilhelm IV, had refused the offer, made to him by the German Liberal Parliament at Frankfurt, of the rule of a constitutional German Liberal state; despite his incessantly wavering sympathies he found it impossible to square his monarchic vows, and his commitment to the imagery of noble society, with any acceptance of even the highest of all dignities at the hands of lesser human beings. Thus the arms of Prussia came to be directed, not against the more predictable 'oppressors', the Austrian empire in Vienna, but against smaller German states, still hesitant between liberal revolution and reaction. The Prussian army prepared to invade Saxony in spring 1849.

Exiled

Wagner had hoped that a Saxon victory could lead to a sense of potential for change, sufficient to inaugurate a republican democratic government of the kind his 1848 manifesto had endorsed. But it was the Prussians who won. Bakunin was arrested, as was Röckel, Wagner's musical and political collaborator. Wagner, by a series of remarkable chances, escaped arrest and made his way rapidly to Weimar and to the hospitality of Liszt, the virtuoso pianist and composer who later became one of Wagner's greatest admirers and most loyal promoters. But Weimar was far too close to Saxony for comfort and Liszt urged Wagner to move outside German territory, to Paris. Wagner's memories of Paris made this an almost unbearable idea; but he briefly passed through Paris in June, hating it as much as before. In July he settled in Zurich.

It was to be thirteen more years before he was allowed to return to German soil. It is notable that Wagner, the radical and even incendiary revolutionary, observed the terms of this prohibition. (Röckel endured the harder fate of thirteen years in prison.) During those years Wagner through his prose writings and (though they were largely unperformed) his musico-dramatic creations was to effect, indeed, a revolution, though in a more limited sphere, and though its full energies were, through Wagner's own deliberate intention, in many ways blunted by the forms of the dramas and the styles of the music in which they were vested. This is not to say that *The Ring* or *Tristan und Isolde*, Wagner's masterpieces of the 1850s, are lesser works because of the maskings of their revolutionary energies. It would be more sensible to see the resulting complexity as an essential part of their greatness.

In 1848 and 1849 Wagner's career had undergone its mid-term crisis. Its resolution was less immediately distressing than might have been expected, and less painful for him than that endured by a number of his friends and associates. On the other hand, Wagner's trials of the 1850s and the early 1860s were remarkably protracted. Perhaps the greatest price that he paid was the frustration produced by a creative life without public acknowledgement. In the years 1849 to 1864 there are remarkably few major landmarks to be found by which any account of his career can be orientated or organized. And this prolonged inactivity and lack of recognition is a mark of many features of his personal life, and certain important elements in the creative work of these years.

In Zurich from 1849, and elsewhere in Switzerland through the 1850s, Wagner was safe from threat of immediate arrest for his participation in the 1849 events in Dresden. By the same token, however, he was under constant Saxon and Imperial police surveillance; all the more because of his friendship with other political radicals in exile in Zurich, including the poet and radical political thinker Georg Herwegh. Herwegh, an important influence on Wagner's thought in the early 1850s, was a friend of Marx and a devotee of the philosophy of Feuerbach, whose influence is prominent in Wagner's important prose writings of these years.

It would have been impossible for Wagner in Swiss territory to secure any musical appointment comparable to that which he had enjoyed in Dresden. In fact his career in the recognised positions open to the leaders of German musical and operatic life was over, a fact his wife Minna was swift to recognise. It was Minna who in the 1850s several times petitioned the new King of Saxony, Johann, for the reinstatement of her husband; she knew well enough what would be required to put both their marriage and any recognizable version of her husband's career back on a firm footing. But no permission was given by the Saxon king.

Wandering musician

Wagner's travels in the 1850s and early 1860s took him to major cities of Europe – Paris, Vienna and Venice – and ultimately further afield still – to Prague, St Petersburg and Moscow. His experience in all these metropolitan centres was that of an outsider, who could never feel emotionally secure, and whose most obvious way of making money and reputation was as a conductor. Extracts from his earlier operas thus could find a hearing, and that hearing was sometimes positive: in Paris in the early months of 1860, and also in London in the course of a generally depressing visit in the spring of 1855, where his music won the appreciation of Queen Victoria and Prince Albert. But any reputation he might acquire in these ways only pinned him all the more to an image, as composer and as human being, which in his mind was becoming increasingly out of date.

The earlier operas achieved very few stage performances in these years, though those performances were, for better or worse, significant. In August 1850 Liszt presided over a production of *Lohengrin* in Weimar. In 1852 Wagner revised *The Flying Dutchman* for a production in Zurich. Above all in 1861 *Tannhäuser* received three performances in Paris. These performances, in a version significantly revised to cater to the Parisian demands for ballet in opera, could have offered Wagner some compensation for his Parisian suffering in the early 1840s, but they were seriously interrupted by hostile demonstrations in the audience. The hostility was directed not so much at Wagner as at Princess Pauline Metternich, the patron of the performances and the wife of the Austrian ambassador, unpopular with radical circles in Paris. Wagner's operas were never to achieve public success in Paris in his lifetime, though before and long after his death many of his most devoted intellectual and musical admirers were to be French artists, composers, writers and thinkers.

Loss of income

Exile involved for Wagner the loss of a public image, as German revolutionary dramatist and musical composer, and of a voice in potential reforms of German cultural and political affairs. It also meant a loss of income, which promised poverty and threatened chronic insolvency. His patrons and supporters in the 1850s deserved his gratitude, and that of all his subsequent admirers. They did not always receive it in any direct or easily recognisable form from Wagner himself. Julie Ritter, widow of a merchant Karl Ritter, had become a friend of Wagner in Dresden, and between 1851 and 1859 supplied him with 800 thalers every year. This fell somewhat short of the 3,000 francs allowance envisaged in 1850 by her and her friend Jessie Laussot, the English wife of a Bordeaux wine merchant. Wagner stayed in Bordeaux with the Laussots in 1850, and his brief affair, and fantasy of elopement, with Jessie, which was thwarted by her mother and her husband, meant the abandonment of the larger plan for financial support.

Debts of 10,000 francs incurred by Wagner up to September 1854 were partly settled at that time by the German businessman Otto Wesendonck, who had retired from his business career to Zurich, and who gained considerable status and self-gratification from his support of Wagner in this and in subsequent years. This support continued even after Wagner's affair (possibly unconsummated) with Otto's wife Mathilde. In 1859, after the ending of the affair, Wagner, returning from Italy, concluded a deal by which Otto bought the copyright of the scores of the four operas comprising the *Ring* cycle (only two of which were as yet complete), and paid 6,000 francs for each score.

Early in 1860 the publisher Schott negotiated for the right to publish Wagner's music, and Wagner offered him the copyright to *Das Rheingold* for a substantial 10,000 francs (then the equivalent of 8,000 marks, or £400; by comparison Verdi, for each of his operas composed between 1847 and 1857 – works including *Rigoletto* and *La Traviata* – received 60,000 francs from his publisher, Ricordi). Wagner's earlier works had had difficulty in finding publication, or terms of publication sufficient to guarantee Wagner's livelihood, let alone to acknowledge the importance he felt due to him and the conditions in which he chose to feel it necessary to work. The Schott deal for *Rheingold* may have been seen by him as a belated acknowledgement of the importance of the *Ring* cycle, and of his whole creative achievement, for the world of German music.

Wagner's negotiations involved a certain amount of duplicity towards both Wesendonck and Schott, which he probably justified to himself on grounds of earlier ill-treatment by the world. This sense of what he felt owing to him emerges again in the extravagant furnishing which he had provided for his lodgings in Vienna in 1863, and more pleasantly in the extravagant gifts he presented to his friends in Christmas of that year. The immediate effect of this was to force him into flight from Vienna, pursued by his Austrian creditors. Financially as in other ways, the early months of 1864 mark one of the lowest points in Wagner's career.

The volume of Wagner's musical and prose output leaves no doubt of his immense vitality, but early physical weaknesses reappeared in more pervasive forms throughout these years of exile. In 1851 he is found undergoing prolonged water cures for erysipelas and constipation. In 1852 depression led him to voice repeated plans of suicide. The erysipelas recurred in 1855. In Venice in early 1859 he was beset with dysentery and by an ulcer on his leg.

The imagery of illness and of healing, frequently by water, can be associated with a number of moments in the *Ring* cycle, in *Tristan und Isolde*, and most obviously in the sufferings, both physical and spiritual, of Amfortas in Wagner's last opera *Parsifal*. Minna Wagner suffered from a bad heart condition,

The Wesendoncks'
Villa on the Grüner
Hügel in Zurich.

which emerged into prominence in the first half of 1854, and
which perhaps led Wagner to prolong their association well
beyond the time when it can have carried much serious
emotional significance for him.

Mathilde Wesendonck

The affair with Jessie Laussot in spring 1850 may well have been
Wagner's first physical relationship outside his marriage. His
intense spiritual and emotional communion with Mathilde
Wesendonck can be traced as far back as late 1854, precisely the
time when her husband's role as benefactor to Wagner began. It
does not seem far-fetched to connect Wagner's liberation from
immediate financial pressure with a sense of emotional release
which led him into these affairs.

In 1857 he set to music five poems by Mathilde, and in this
and the next year her return of his feelings led the complicated
relations between the Wagners and the Wesendoncks to the
point where Wagner felt it necessary to withdraw, first to Paris,
and then, after a crisis in April caused by Minna's reading of a
letter from him to Mathilde, to Venice. His return to Switzerland
in 1859, which led to the new business arrangements with Otto
Wesendonck, was followed by two years largely spent in Paris,
to which Minna followed him in November 1859. These years
were the final attempt by the Wagners to sustain their marriage
relationship. The failure of *Tannhäuser* led Richard inevitably to

new attempts at self-definition, outside the conventions of the Parisian stage and also outside the limits of his marriage. A further crisis in February 1862, when Wagner was staying in Biebrich on the Rhine, was described by him as 'ten days in hell'. From this time onwards Minna and Wagner were to live apart. He met her for the last time in November in Dresden in 1862.

In July of 1862 he re-encountered the woman who was to replace Minna as his wife; Cosima, the daughter of Liszt and by now the wife of the German composer and conductor Hans von Bülow. Wagner had met Cosima in 1853 on a brief visit to Paris, when she was fifteen, and the Wagners and also the Wesendoncks had been visited by Cosima and Hans in Lucerne in autumn 1857. The relationship between Wagner and Cosima reached an emotional climax of commitment in November 1863. By the time it was physically consummated, Wagner's conditions in other ways had undergone the most extreme change.

Wagner's financial precariousness can be seen as an influence in his emotional restlessness and mobility in these years. Both were, in turn, fuelled by his exile and by the requirement of frequent travel, and contacts with new people and new societies. Minna had been wise in her own interests to appeal to the King of Saxony in 1854 for clemency and reinstatement for her husband, though in the early 1850s Wagner's intellectual commitment to revolutionary solutions for German politics was by no means abandoned, and the King's refusal to reinstate Wagner was well founded. As late as 1859 Wagner, staying in Venice during the composition of *Tristan und Isolde*, underwent regular police surveillance from the agents of the Austrian emperor (in whose territory at this time Venice still lay); the experience of watchfulness and betrayal undergone by the adulterous lovers, in the second act of that opera, may correspond to Wagner's sense of involvement in a potentially adulterous love affair with Mathilde Wesendonck which brought upon him the enmity not only of a husband but also of a state.

In August 1860 Wagner was permitted to return to the German states (though not to Saxony until 1862). Wagner's last meeting with Minna in November 1862 in Dresden also symbolised his final rejection of a Saxon, and stable, musical career. His residence in Vienna in 1863, which led him into considerable debts, may have seen him attempting, however subconsciously, to fulfil the conditions of life due to a genius in an imperial capital. It was a political change which was to bring about the end to this second prolonged period of wandering, and to install Wagner at the heart of a kingdom and at the ear of a king.

Prose writings

The first creative fruits of Wagner's years of exile were his prose writings. In 1849 he composed *Art and Revolution* and *The Art Work of the Future*. In 1850 these were followed by *Jewishness in Music* and by the bulk of *Opera and Drama*, completed early in 1851. In 1851 he also completed *A Communication to my Friends*. In these increasingly extended tracts he pursued important, complex and sometimes confused trains of thought, concerning German music, German opera and above all the relations between word, theme and music in what he came to designate no longer as opera but as music drama. This involved Wagner in coming to terms with what seemed to him of greatest significance in his operas of the 1840s, and with sketching the direction in which both logic and his own creative wishes suggested his style should develop. Wagner is thus theorising ahead of the evidence. The viability and value of his theories rests on the early works of the *Ring* cycle, *Das Rheingold*, *Die Walküre* and to some extent *Siegfried*. These were slow to emerge; a complicated process of prose and verse sketches and scenarios preceded actual musical composition.

Already in 1848, Wagner had completed a prose scenario entitled 'The Nibelung Myth'. This sketch led to a libretto, entitled *Siegfried's Tod* ('The Death of Siegfried'), which in November 1848 Wagner read to a group of friends. This turned into *Götterdämmerung* (The Twilight of the Gods). But Wagner came to feel that too much narrative was presupposed in this text, and that it would be necessary to dramatise the events preceding Siegfried's death. In 1850 he began sketching music for the 1848 libretto, but was driven to add first a scenario, then a verse libretto for a new work to be entitled 'Young Siegfried'. A similar process of reconstruction from narration to direct dramatic enactment led him, before the end of 1851, to develop prose sketches for the operas *Das Rheingold* and *Die Walküre*, which he turned into verse in 1852. His acceptance of the consequent four-part structure for the *Ring* necessitated revision of the previous texts of 'Young Siegfried' and 'Siegfried's Death'. In February 1853 the *Ring* poem was complete. Wagner had it published in an edition of fifty copies and read it to an invited audience in a Zurich hotel. There were to be subsequent changes to the texts, but from this point onwards the dramatic outlines of the cycle were firmly established.

Wagner had produced no new opera for five years, since the completion of *Lohengrin* in 1848. They had been years of excitement, but more of frustration, disappointment and perhaps self-reproach. It is perhaps the greatest triumph of tenacity in the whole of his career that he forthwith set himself to the entire musical composition of the four poetic texts which he had created. This was bound to be an even more protracted task. It would have been rash to expect it to last less than five years. In fact, it lasted twenty-one years.

Composing the *Ring*

Musical drafts for *Das Rheingold* were begun by the end of 1853. The composition of *Die Walküre* occupied Wagner between 1854 and 1856 and he proceeded with *Siegfried* until August 1857. This is a notably rapid pace of composition, given Wagner's emotional and financial involvements, and his conducting commitments in London and elsewhere. Any discouragement at the resounding silence into which his fame as a composer had fallen would be understandable, and it was perhaps the felt need to complete a work, albeit on (at least in his intention) a smaller scale, which led him away from the *Ring* into the writing and composition of *Tristan und Isolde*. On the other hand, there is no doubt that *Tristan und Isolde* was conceived by Wagner in relation to two other powerful stimuli; one was his involvement with Mathilde Wesendonck; the other, though hard to evaluate, was his encounter with the philosophy of Arthur Schopenhauer.

Wagner's first conception of *Tristan und Isolde* dates from the end of 1854. The earliest datable sketches of it are from December 1856. After breaking off the composition of *Siegfried* in August 1857, Wagner began work on *Tristan* and continued it through the travels and emotional excitements of 1858 and 1859 with astounding speed, intensity and concentration. Of all Wagner's scores *Tristan* is the most revolutionary, and the most subtly unified, in its musical language, and in both these respects it stands at an opposite pole from Wagner's other supreme but profoundly incommensurable masterpiece, the *Ring* cycle.

Tristan und Isolde thus marks the most significant and identifiable product of these fifteen years of exile, deprivation and self-imposed emotional sufferings. There were other compositions: for example, a piano sonata for Mathilde Wesendonck in the spring of 1853, a revision of what now became known as the *Faust overture* early in 1855, and a setting of five poems by Mathilde, now known as the *Wesendonck-Lieder*, in 1857. Their musical language shows similarities to, and echoes of, the style of *Tristan und Isolde*.

The idea of an opera based on the legends surrounding the hero Parzifal emerges in 1857. Late in 1861 Wagner began work on the writing of *Die Meistersinger*. He read the poetic form of its libretto in February 1862 in Mainz to various friends, and again in November 1862 in Vienna, where the musical critic Eduard Hanslick rightly perceived that Wagner's character Beckmesser (earlier 'Hanslich') was an outrageous and vicious lampoon on his own character and views, and left the reading.

All this activity, sometimes sporadic, often concentrated and intense, in the fields of prose writing, poetic re-writing and musical composition was accompanied by periods in which Wagner, out of financial necessity, but also driven by his own need for public recognition, undertook the conducting of individual concerts or series of concerts: in Zurich in May 1853, in London throughout the spring of 1855, in Paris early in 1860, and, throughout much of 1863, in Prague, St Petersburg and Moscow, Budapest, Karlsruhe, Breslau and Vienna.

Wagner's conducting was noted, but not always admired, for the extent to which he appeared as fellow-composer in the act of performance. One sign of this, which became a Wagnerian trademark, was the extent to which he adopted large changes of tempo in the course of a single movement, despite the lack of any such marking in the score. By such dramatisation of symphonic structures, Wagner left his mark on the subsequent history of musical performance.

Wagner's isolation in these years was mitigated by two friendships, of different significance. Liszt's championship of *Lohengrin* in Weimar in 1850 led to his visiting Wagner in 1853, when Wagner read the score of Liszt's *Faust symphony*, and in 1856, when Wagner was able to study Liszt's symphonic poems. Wagner's revision of his *Faust overture* seems likely to have been connected with these encounters, and his belief in common ground between the Germanic symphony and his own distinctive conceptions of music-drama is likely to have appeared vindicated through the friendship.

Berlioz and Wagner met in London in 1855; each could sympathise with the other's frustration at the lack of interest displayed by their own national audiences. Back in Paris in 1858 on a brief visit, Wagner had Berlioz read to him the text of his epic operatic masterpiece *Les Troyens* (The Trojans). Wagner will have realised, as Berlioz could not yet realise, the gulf separating their conceptions of historical epic. Wagner was driven, at least consciously, to overcome separations between word and music, between one and another character. Berlioz's work thrives on the constant separation of forms, images, perceptions and characters from one another. Moreover, where Wagner can be seen, in these years, condemned to isolation, but seeking, often desperately, to escape it by contact with audiences and lovers, Berlioz can be seen, throughout his career and in *Les Troyens* above all, as embracing an isolation both necessary and productive.

Wagner and Schopenhauer
Will, Representation and Music

It is tempting to identify Wagner's reading of Schopenhauer's philosophical masterpiece *The World as Will and Representation* in September and October 1854 as the hitherto unrecognised great landmark in these years of exile, disturbance and passion. Wagner was introduced to Schopenhauer's work by Herwegh, and letters in 1854 and 1855 certainly testify to Wagner's will to be impressed by Schopenhauer as he understood him. To Liszt in December 1854 Wagner wrote:

'I have now become exclusively preoccupied with a man, who – albeit only in literary form – has entered my lonely life like a gift from heaven. It is Arthur Schopenhauer, the greatest philosopher since Kant . . . The German professors have – very wisely – ignored him for forty years. He was recently rediscovered – to Germany's shame – by an English critic . . . His principal idea, the final denial of the will to live, is of terrible seriousness, but it is uniquely redeeming. Of course it did not strike me as anything new, and nobody can think such a thought if he has not already lived it. But it was this philosopher who first awakened the idea in me with such clarity. When I think back on the storms which have buffeted my heart and on its convulsive efforts to cling to some hopes in life – against my own better judgement – indeed, now that these storms have swelled so often to the fury of a tempest – I have yet found a sedative which has finally helped me sleep at night; it is the sincere and heartfelt yearning for death; total unconsciousness, complete annihilation, the end of all dreams, the only ultimate redemption . . .

For the sake of young Siegfried, the fairest of my life's dreams, I expect that I must still complete the Nibelung pieces   . . . But it will be 1856 before I have completed the whole thing, and 1858 . . . before I can perform it – if fate so decrees. But since I have never in my life enjoyed the true happiness of love, I intend to erect a further monument to this most beautiful of dreams, a monument in which this love will be properly sated from beginning to end: I have planned in my head a *Tristan und Isolde*, the simplest but most full-blooded musical conception; with the 'black flag' which flutters at the end, I shall then cover myself over, in order – to die.'

Wagner and Schopenhauer never met. Schopenhauer's masterpiece had been written more than thirty-five years earlier. Schopenhauer's often virulent attacks on women and on sexual love indicate the size of the gulf between his and Wagner's overt preoccupations and, as Wagner realised, no figure could be further from Schopenhauer's ideas than 'Young Siegfried'. Schopenhauer was sent a copy of the *Ring* text by Wagner: he hated it.

Much of this may be beside the point. Wagner was never a professional philosopher; on the other hand his misunderstandings, or conscious misappropriations, of philosophy frequently serve well the purposes of music-dramas which have rightly stimulated philosophical attention. Moreover, Schopenhauer's work is in some respects at odds with itself, thus inviting partial and fruitfully tendentious re-workings.

It may be said that Wagner took from Schopenhauer a vindication of his own feelings in the 1850s: exhaustion, frustration and guilt. Wagner characterises Schopenhauer's philosophy as denying the will to live. Schopenhauer is in fact concerned, rather, to characterise all the objects of human understanding, the whole world as we represent it to ourselves, as a set of manifestations, in different degrees, with different kinds of clarity or obscurity, of the will to live. We ourselves as individual and social human beings demonstrate, despite our own ignorance of the fact, this will. Such a will, in the natural and human world, appears in the forms of miserable and perpetual struggle; what Iris Murdoch characterises as 'restless desire and ruthless egotistic striving' (*Metaphysics as a Guide to Morals*). This – the grim, near-inescapable coherence of all we do and experience – is what we do not know about ourselves; and our ignorance confirms us in our disastrous and almost irremediable suffering.

The bleakness of Schopenhauer's conception is, in his philosophical system, mitigated by the perceivable empirical human instinct of compassion; ultimately it may be eliminated by a very thorough-going denial of the will, and it is of this that Wagner seems to speak in his letter to Liszt. But what Schopenhauer has in mind is (quite consciously) much closer to a Buddhist notion of asceticism, involving a denial of the reality and significance of all physical and temporal experience, than Wagner seems to have appreciated. Schopenhauer's challenge here is to the perpetual self-delusions in which Western would-be aesthetic and social critics involve themselves.

For Schopenhauer indeed there is a third path by which the operations of the will may in some part be understood and its effects mitigated or resisted. This is the path leading through forms and disciplines of art. It has frequently been supposed, particularly by musicians and musical commentators on Wagner, that the supremacy accorded by Schopenhauer to music consists in the ability of music and of the musical composer, more fully than any other artist, to fulfil the general function which Schopenhauer assigns to art; to offer, by its structure rather than by objective reference, some manifestation of the world as it really is.

This is some way from Schopenhauer's own view of music. Schopenhauer writes that 'music is by no means like the other arts, a copy of ideas, but a copy of the will itself whose objectivity the ideas are' (*The*

Arthur Schopenhauer, 1788-1860. Much of his philosophical work was done in Wagner's youth, but Wagner read him first in autumn 1854.

World as Will and Representation, book 3, section 52). Schopenhauer ascribes to music not a function of representation (that is, in 'ideas'), but of conveying, in a manner more direct than representation or ideas, the operations of the will itself. Elsewhere Schopenhauer writes, with reference to traditional classical and romantic music, 'what resists our apprehen-sion, the irrational relation or dissonance, becomes the natural type of what resists our will'.

One can gather from this that Schopenhauer's sense of the rest-lessness of the will, and of perpetual endless struggle which he sees as the operation of the will, may itself in turn have been modelled on certain features of classical and romantic music. The more general philosophical point here is that music precisely does not, as the other arts may to some extent do, banish or distance the force and the desires of the human ego; rather music soothes the ego, by embodying in its own operations the closest contact, though not an intellectual contact, with the manner in which the will, the ego, exists.

Insofar then as Wagner identified something genuine in Schopenhauer's philosophy by the phrase 'denial of the will to live', he would have been right to paraphrase this as a *denial* of music. But clearly Wagner drew no such conclusion. Indeed the subordination of music to word and dramatic theme, which is a characteristic of Wagner's aesthetic prose writings of the very early 1850s, gives way in Wagner's actual compositions of the mid and late 1850s to a new degree of centrality for specifically musical processes. And these processes, seen above all in *Tristan und Isolde*, involve a melodic, harmonic and emotional language which is, in Schopenhauerian terms, supremely 'wilful', full of 'restless desire and ruthless egotistical striving'. It is, then, Schopenhauer's conception of the 'will to live' which inspires Wagner's 'simplest but most full-blooded musical conception', rather than the 'denial' of such a will.

If it were to be argued that the drama of *Tristan und Isolde* expressed 'denial', and thus coincided with Schopenhauer's personal predilections for asceticism, escape and death, then to that extent the drama and the music of *Tristan* would be profoundly at odds with one another. In being so, they would translate into their own musico-dramatic medium a tension central to Schopenhauer's thought. On such a view the exact degree of Wagner's conscious understanding of Schopenhauer's explicit philosophy would become almost impossible, and perhaps unimportant, to determine. And such tensions, within both the aesthetic elements and the conceptual structures of Wagner's music-dramas, offer a basis for identifying not their failure but their greatness.

The Schopenhauerian connection of perpetual egoistic struggle with the will to live relates interestingly to the dramaturgy of *Rienzi* and *Lohengrin* in particular. If *Lohengrin* is a tragedy in which projects of social regeneration encounter and destroy one another, and are also destroyed by the inadequacy of that society which they seek to reform; then a Schopenhauerian conception of individual and social life does considerable justice to this dramaturgy. Wagner had much on his side when, in the letter to Liszt already quoted, he claims to have already experienced, in his own life indeed, but also in his art, those conceptions and pressures which his intellectual encounter with Schopenhauer brought to a more complete self-consciousness.

Chapter 5

Theories and Music Dramas: 1848-1861

Wagner wrote prose concerning music-drama, philosophy, history and politics for most of his active life. The most significant parts of this output are concentrated in two periods. The first was the early years of exile, the late 1840s and early 1850s. The second was the last seven years of his life, after the performance of the *Ring* at Bayreuth in 1876. Of these two major bodies of theoretical prose, the first is by far the more conceptually intricate, theoretically ambitious and intellectually stimulating. It is unfortunate that the second had a significantly larger influence on Wagner's disciples during the last years of his life, and for decades after his death. In what follows, I shall attempt to interpret the train of thought which guides Wagner through the four or more major works of the early exile years.

Wagner's thinking concerning drama, music and their audience orientates itself from the model of ancient Athenian drama, which included both tragedy and comedy. Wagner's remarks seem largely to have had Greek tragedy in mind, but their relevance to ancient comedy, and their bearing on his mature comedy, *Die Meistersinger*, are also worth considering.

Wagner's conception of Athenian tragedy rested on the unity that, in his view, it achieved between a large number of different artistic media – speech in verse, music, design, dance and acting. He believed that the mythical narratives employed by Athenian tragic playwrights were essential to the nature of this drama, and equally that the presence of very large audiences unified, not by rank or wealth, but simply by membership of the Athenian democracy, was crucial to the drama's nature and success. He argued that the decline of Athenian tragedy consisted in the separating out of its several component arts from one another. He saw it as his mission to reveal this separation as merely a temporary falling-off; in his view, Athenian national drama could in his time be re-created as a universal music-drama. And, though for him the German nation, German culture and the German language were the necessary tools with which to create such a drama, nonetheless, in his thought, the audience for such a drama would be world-wide; other nations (within certain important limits), could imitate such drama in their own languages and within their own national cultures.

The limit on this conception lay, in his view, in the nature of Judaism and in the position of the Jews in nineteenth-century European society. For Wagner, Jews were unable properly to speak, and therefore still more unable artistically to express themselves, in any contemporary European language; they were capable only of mimicry, whose artificiality betrayed itself by the inorganic and arbitrary relations set up in Jewish artistic works between form and content. But what in Wagner's view was an endemic disease, affecting all Jewish attempts at self-expression or collective expression, had also become, he thought, a modern, post-Renaissance condition, affecting, above all, the art known as opera.

Wagner equated the nature of opera, as traditionally understood, with the aria, that is the form of extended, frequently elaborate, melodic song, which dominated Italian opera in the seventeenth and eighteenth centuries, and which prevailed, though less overwhelmingly, in French opera of the same periods. In Wagner's view, Rossini's achievement amounted to a brilliant reduction of such aria-based opera to its fundamental elements. Weber, much admired by Wagner, had sought to integrate his operas on the basis of the domination of melody, and in consequence had fallen victim both to the inadequacy of the texts with which his librettists provided him, and to the inherent impossibility of generating a coherent relation between music and drama on the basis of melody alone. Wagner saw this failure as bearing witness to the problems arising generally within the realm claimed by opera; the realm in which music, words, dance, design and an underlying dramatic theme constantly, laboriously and sometimes violently waged war upon one another, each seeking to enslave the other to its own purposes.

Artistic unity
Wagner's mission was to supersede this state of general artistic warfare, with artistic unity; that is with the ideal of the '*Gesamtkunstwerk*' – the total unified work of art. What might this involve? Logically, that no one medium of artistic expression should dominate over any other; melody, and the demands of singers, should not dictate, in advance, the nature of the verse or of the dramatic theme; nor (logically) should a dramatic theme determine the style or harmonic content of the

music. Such 'non-determination' might logically be expressed by an ideal not of unification, but of separation, between artistic elements, coupled with a will, on the parts of each of the several creative artists involved, to respect one another's competence, and the inherent limitations of each other's media.

But this, it is clear, was not Wagner's conception. He had in mind not a democracy of artistic media, but a logical sequence whereby the (necessary) determining effect of one medium on another could be rationalised, understood and made acceptable.

Wagner never entered into a relationship between himself, as composer, and any writer, as librettist. When, at Bayreuth, he was in a position to realise his conceptions in practice, he revealed himself more than willing, and in some ways more than competent, to deploy hitherto unrealised skills; as stage director, even, to some extent, as participant in the art of design for the stage. Thus the non-democratic nature of Wagner's conception emerges with some clarity.

But one can vindicate the sincerity of his position by presenting the logical processes with which he sought to articulate the unity he desired. In one version of Wagnerian theory, what comes first is the verse. Wagner had detailed proposals for revolution in the nature of musico-dramatic verse, implemented in *Das Rheingold* and throughout the *Ring*. The rhyme and regular metre of traditional operatic verse were to be replaced by alliterative verse, in which stress, rather than rhyme, determined the nature of the poetry, with a constantly changing number of syllables employed in successive lines. Such verse, a medium new to opera, was a basic mode in medieval German (and English) verse, sometimes combined with rhyme. In his view this was notably less artificial than traditional rhymed forms of poetry, and nearer to ordinary speech. Wagner's arguments here are powerful, and anticipate features of later verse revolutions, introduced independently in German and in other Northern European traditions, whose speech patterns are largely dominated by local stress. Alliterative verse confers upon the music dramas of the *Ring* the considerable degree of conversational flexibility which their characters display, both in monologue and in frequent argument.

If this new style of verse was to be taken as the origin of the new music drama, the melodic language of the music would adapt to the verse, rather than follow any predetermined symmetrical patterns; in turn, though more remotely, a number of changes in the deployment of harmonic sequences and cadences might be expected. Wagner developed this line of thought, but in his theories a different argument runs in parallel with this.

According to this second view, the foundation of the new style is the continuity of the orchestral writing; words and vocal melody are to be understood as superimposed upon the orchestra, and determined, conceptually and melodically, by the sequence of orchestral themes. In a more extreme view, melody and words alike are to be understood as local, even arbitrary, instances of a more fundamental, wordless drama, enacted in the orchestral writing, and intelligible in terms of symphonic procedures, procedures of thematic exposition, development and re-presentation, standing in a complex but definable relation to those of the symphony, above all to the symphonies of Beethoven.

The Leitmotif

It is in relation to this argument that the notion of the '*Motif*', or 'Leitmotif' (the theme, or the leading theme) came to assume the importance that it did.

A motif is a recognisable musical theme; frequently very brief, frequently harmonically and rhythmically simple, in any case identifiable when it recurs, and when it is modified in its recurrences. Its first presentation is associated with a character, an object, a dramatic situation, a relationship between characters or (in some of the most significant but most elusive cases) a thematic concept of relevance to large tracts of the musical drama. Very many leitmotifs may be identified in the *Ring*. Many of them bear close resemblances to one another, and the orchestral elaboration of individual themes increasingly connects them. It is this web of developmental, often contrapuntal, writing which amounts to the practical justification for seeing the orchestra rather than the verse as the basis of Wagnerian music drama.

In yet another view, neither verse nor orchestra would be the determining feature of such music drama. Rather, the 'drama' itself would guarantee the appropriateness of the verse and render intelligible the web of motivic orchestral writing. To put this another way might be to say, simply, that each separate music drama, from *Das Rheingold* onwards, presents certain general themes and coherent arguments, through specific human relationships; an uncontentious claim perhaps, but not one characteristically advanced by earlier composers of opera, nor indeed one on whose details it would be easy to obtain unanimous critical agreement with respect to the works concerned. Nonetheless, as with major works of fiction, poetry or drama employing purely verbal media, so with Wagner's operas, it seems entirely appropriate that one should seek interpretations in terms of some convergence of separate themes upon a central set of concerns and a persuasive argument around these concerns.

Wagner during the composition of *Tristan und Isolde*; greatness and suffering.

For Wagner, a mythological subject was the preferred dramatic theme, given its power to focus the concerns of a nation, or indeed of a long national and (in his view) racial tradition. But he frequently professed less concern with the specific story lines preserved in traditional narrative, and far more interest in the contemporary human and social issues to which such narratives could be seen symbolically to refer. The tension between mythological narrative and symbolic connotation pervades all Wagner's music-dramas, though in different measure and through different practices of signification.

Some works, such as *Das Rheingold*, can best be understood as rather specific allegories; here the details of the narrative, and their intended meanings, can be seen as separate and, by the same token, susceptible of fairly straightforward equation, one with another. In other dramas, even within the *Ring*, we are presented not so much with allegory as with action which can be taken as exemplary for a wide variety of human, and therefore contemporary, situations. In other works again, (*Parsifal* and arguably *Die Meistersinger*) we are presented with narratives which demand from their audiences not only the attention offered to artistic or intellectual interpretation, but also that proper to religious or ritual participation. Thus Wagner's stress on mythological subjects conceals radical differences in his subsequent uses of them; differences to which neither he nor subsequent interpreters have done sufficient justice.

This body of theory bears many marks of the place and time of its conception. It is the theory of an exile, calling out beyond his immediate circumstances to the German states, and ultimately to the single German state, which his creative needs demand. Beyond even such a nationalistic appeal, it is not hard to discern a universal appeal of the kind that might be expected of a German composer of music, whose art could glory in its national tradition, but also postulate an audience unlimited by any boundaries, even of language.

Secondly, the theory is a demand for revolution rather than for reform. However much the practice of earlier Wagnerian opera (and opera in general) can still be discerned in subsequent Wagnerian music-drama, and, I would argue, advantageously discerned, nonetheless the intentional significance of the break created, within Wagner's practice, by this body of theory must not be under-estimated. A new version of operatic language is offered, dismantling the traditions of the aria and absorbing the practice of the recitative while radically transforming its mode. The vehicle for this transformation is the orchestra; and while the Wagnerian orchestra is composed of a great number of instrumentalists and a great variety of instruments, the notion of orchestral unity confers upon the theory an appearance of intellectual unity and originality. Thus, the sharp difference between the orchestral sounds of Wagner and of Berlioz can be directly related to their respective dramatic psychologies, both social and collective. Wagner's characters seek unification, within themselves and with social wholes, whereas Berlioz's characters, whatever their social position, constantly experience their lot as one of isolation and self-division whether heroic or tragic.

Finally, Wagner's theories involve a passionate but ambivalent appeal to audiences. Audiences were what Wagner, now and for many years afterwards, lacked. Inevitably he was driven to seek an audience both heterogeneous and coherent. A coherent audience would understand the logical thrust of his theories and their inter-relation, and could be expected emotionally to respond to the resulting works with the integrated affect which Wagner claimed to find in Athenian audiences faced by Athenian tragedy. On the other hand, under existing circumstances, as Wagner realised, different audiences, from different national cultural traditions, posed different demands and expectations;

and, as perhaps Wagner never sufficiently took into account, even a German audience was, and for the foreseeable future would be, divided by factors of age, class, status and gender in ways which would make its response to Wagnerian music drama, if not unpredictable, at least divided and divisive.

Das Rheingold: *Plot*

The first scene is set in the depths of the river Rhine. Three Rhine maidens are playing in the waves. One of them, Flosshilde, urges her sisters to keep guard over the gold, which it is their duty to watch. Alberich the dwarf ogles them as they play. They hate his appearance but flirt with him. Realising he has been deceived, he cries out in frustration. The waters of the river are illuminated by the sun which calls forth a gleam of gold from the rock in the middle of the waves. The maidens sing in greeting to the gold and joyfully swim around it. Alberich asks them what it is. They tell him it is the Rhinegold. From it a ring can be made which will give infinite power to the one who makes and wears it. But it can only be fashioned by one willing to abandon all feelings of love and all hope of love returned. Alberich, already frustrated in love, climbs on to the rock, seizes the gold and bears it away with him to his subterranean caves.

The scene changes to a mountain height, on which Wotan, the chief of the gods, and Fricka, his consort, are asleep. Behind them a fortress is illuminated by the rays of the rising sun. Wotan praises his own achievement of having the fortress built. Fricka reminds him of the debt for its building, owed to the giants who constructed it; that is, Freia, their sister, the Goddess of Love. She blames his willingness to give up beauty and love for the security that the fortress represents. He promises that he has no intention of giving up their sister. But she now arrives, in flight from the giants, who swiftly follow her, claiming their reward. Wotan mocks their ugliness, and frets as he awaits the arrival of Loge, the God of Fire, who has promised to relieve him of his bond. The giants remind him of his obligation to preserve treaties, which is symbolised by his spear. Fasolt, one of the giants, loves Freia; his brother Fafner desires the power her abduction from the gods will guarantee for the giants.

Donner and Froh, brothers of the other gods, threaten the giants with force. Wotan acknowledges that force will not resolve the situation. At last Loge arrives. He has found that the fortress meets all stipulations: thus, the letter of the contract must be observed. Wotan asks Loge if he has discovered any substitute with which to pay the giants. He explains that in all his travels around the world he has found nothing that anyone is willing to accept in exchange for love. The only exception is

Alberich, who has bartered away the possibility of love in exchange for gold and for the ring of power.

The giants and Wotan realise the implications. Wotan longs to gain the ring for himself. Loge warns that it should be restored to the Rhine maidens themselves, and suggests that it be stolen from the dwarf. The giants provisionally accept the ring and the gold as substitute for Freia, but meanwhile keep her as a guarantee. As they drag her away, a shadow of old age passes over the immortal youthful beauty of the gods. Loge mockingly draws attention to this, adding that he himself is only half a god and thus scarcely suffers as they do. Wotan urges Loge to descend with him to the caves of the dwarf, promising that he will return with the gold.

The third scene takes place in Alberich's realm of Nibelheim. He has ordered his brother Mime to manufacture from the gold a magic helmet (the Tarnhelm) which transforms or makes invisible the wearer. Alberich puts it on to test Mime's workmanship; he becomes invisible, beats Mime and leaves in triumph. Wotan and Loge arrive. Loge offers to defend Mime and his fellow dwarfs, and Mime explains how the Nibelung blacksmiths had been enslaved by Alberich. Alberich returns, followed by his slaves, who heap up his gold. He challenges the gods to tell him why they have come, and boasts of the power he has gained by the forfeiture of love. One day, he threatens, he will rise from the depths, overcoming the gods and abducting the goddesses. Loge asks how he would defend himself, meanwhile, against a thief. Alberich explains the power of the magic helmet. He shows himself, first, as a dragon; Loge pretends extreme terror at the sight; next, as a tiny toad crawling over the rocks – and the gods bind him with ropes, dragging him away with them as they return to the mountain heights on which the fourth and final scene is set.

They mock Alberich's dreams of world conquest, and invite him to save himself by surrendering the gold. Alberich calculates that if he can retain the helmet, or, in the last resort, only the ring, he can still regain all he may temporarily lose. He calls the slaves to bring the gold, and they pile it around him. He demands the helmet back from the gods; Loge mockingly refuses it and adds it to the pile. Wotan now asks Alberich for the ring. Alberich refuses it. Wotan reminds him that it was not his, but the property of the Rhinemaidens. Alberich in turn reminds Wotan of the price he has paid to gain it, and of the universal crime which Wotan's theft of it would constitute. Wotan, undeterred, tears the ring from Alberich's fingers. Alberich lays a curse upon the ring and all who will subsequently possess it.

Wotan and Loge are welcomed back by the other gods. The giants return with Freia. Fasolt insists that he can only give up

Freia if the gold is piled around her, rendering her invisible to him. Loge and Froh pile up the gold. Fafner can still see Freia's hair, and the helmet is thrown onto the pile. Fasolt can see her eyes, and the giants demand the ring to stop up the crack in the hoard. Wotan refuses to yield the ring; Loge urges again the claim of the maidens upon it, but Wotan resists all appeals, until Erda, the Goddess of the Earth, warns him of the power of the curse, and the doom faced by him and all the gods unless he surrenders it. Wotan obeys her and surrenders the ring.

The giants begin to take the gold away, but quarrel over it; and Fafner, reminding Fasolt that he had loved Freia more than the gold, kills him. Wotan sees the curse already taking effect. After thunder and lightening summoned by Donner, the God of Storm, a bridge formed by a rainbow leads the gods into their fortress, Valhalla. Loge, watching, tells of how they are hastening to their end. He will detach himself from them and transform himself back into his element of fire. As the gods cross the bridge the maidens from the depths below sing sadly of their loss of the gold.

Das Rheingold: *Commentary*

Many elements in the compact and well-knit narrative of this opera were created by Wagner on the basis of little or nothing in the complex sources, but he fashioned them into a remarkably coherent structure. The Rhinemaidens are Wagner's creation entirely; for the link between Loge and the element of fire Wagner had only Jacob Grimm as his source. Wagner made the Goddess Fricka into the conservative conscience of her consort Wotan. Above all he set up the parallelism between the renunciations of love accomplished by Alberich and, at least temporarily, by Wotan. One effect of this parallelism is to tie up a number of otherwise loose ends in the mythological basis for the opera and for those three operas which follow it in the *Ring* cycle. But another effect is to allow Wagner, in those three subsequent operas, to develop freely a number of human stories proceeding from the basis of this tightly constructed allegory of gods, goddesses, giants, dwarfs and Rhinemaidens.

Thus in some ways *Das Rheingold* is a misleading beginning to the cycle which follows it. On the basis of *Das Rheingold*, one would expect a cycle concerned with conflict between Alberich and the gods, and with the ultimate destination of the ring. But, though Alberich returns in *Siegfried* and *Götterdämmerung*, the contest between the gods and Alberich has slipped far into the background by the end of the cycle. Furthermore the antithesis, in *Das Rheingold*, between the innocence of nature and the Rhinemaidens and the possibilities of power gained by revenge and malice, is a simplification of, rather than a guide for, the moral worlds of the subsequent dramas.

In many ways *Das Rheingold* dramatises clarification; a central theme of it is the way in which that which is concealed is brought to the light. The gold is brought out of the depths of the river, Alberich's dreams of domination are exposed to the clear light of day, and Alberich's claims against the gods and their hypocrisy are allowed to resonate with full force. Alberich's power is shown to be gained as a result of the operation of shame and the demand for revenge, but such a pattern of concealment and its consequent emotions is seen to be not unique to him but equally to pervade the moral world of characters from such different species as giants and gods. Thus the apparent clarity of *Das Rheingold* itself conceals far-reaching complexities.

Das Rheingold lacks, on the face of it, a hero, and certainly Wagner's deployment of vocal types involved no necessity for the heroic tenor voice which was to emerge in all his subsequent operas. Loge's role requires a different kind of tenor voice, capable of both warm lyricism and acrid clarity; he could be seen as the intellectual and (differently) moral focus of the work. Intellectually it is he who spells out with maximum clarity, for gods and giants alike, the possibilities and the risks of gaining the ring; it is also he who most strikingly urges the moral claim of the Rhinemaidens to it. He can be seen as a spokesperson, both for the claims of power and for those of love; and the poise between them, which his character establishes, a poise achieved by the operation of a disinterested and somewhat malevolent intelligence, is one attained by no character in the whole of the subsequent cycle – not even Brünnhilde at its end.

The clarity of action in *Das Rheingold* is matched by the clarity with which a very large number of themes, associated with characters, objects, issues and processes of action, is expounded by the singers and by the orchestra. In *Das Rheingold* most of these motifs are presented straightforwardly and separately from one another, whether on voices or in the orchestra. In subsequent operas they are woven together in increasingly complex counterpoints.

But already in *Das Rheingold* the listener can trace the crucial process by which a theme passes over into another. Thus the theme of the gold appearing in the waters, in the first scene, passes over into the lament of the maidens at the end of the drama; this in turn three operas later will be transformed into a theme linked to Hagen's greed for the ring. The motif associated with the ring closely resembles that heard at the first appearance of the fortress Valhalla, indicating the connection (which the narrative has yet to make) between the building of the castle and the necessity of payment for it. Other prominent themes are associated with the waves of the river; with the element of fire, and the critical play of Loge's intelligence; with the hammering of the dwarfs who shape goods out of the Rhinegold; with the treaties to which Wotan has bound himself and, perhaps most prominently of all, with the curse placed by Alberich upon the ring.

These themes, in *Das Rheingold* and in subsequent operas, show a certain tendency to recur in their original key. Many of the most powerful moments in the opera are of great harmonic simplicity: for example the opening, when a single chord of E flat major is sustained for well over one hundred bars of increasing volume and complexity of orchestral texture, as we are given an impression of the depths of the river and (perhaps) the origins of life; the moment when the sun illuminates the gold in the water, as a chord of C major takes shape through the play of harmony; the first announcement of the Valhalla theme at the start of the second scene; and the procession of the gods into Valhalla. But much of the work is in a succession of minor keys.

There are very few separable musical numbers for solo voices. *Das Rheingold* is a work largely given over to conversation, regularly combative and violent in tone, between individual characters; only the three Rhinemaidens sing as a group. In this respect the work shows close resemblances to *Lohengrin*. The great difference between them is the increased flexibility of rhythm achieved in *Das Rheingold*. Wagner gains this partly by a subtle alternation between time-signatures, the 4/4 passages being associated with dramatic conflict.

But above all it is the new verse style of *Das Rheingold's* text which gives, to the later work and to most of the *Ring* cycle, its unique flexibility of verbal rhythm. This in turn lends to the musical rhythms the subtlety with which they register the play of characters and of conflict. Wagner's poetry has abandoned rhyme, and avoids any regularity of length between successive lines. Instead, as we have already noted, it is organised by the principle of alliteration, with every line offering at least two strongly stressed alliterative words. Within this principle the number of syllables in successive lines is largely a matter of indifference. Thus a certain regularity of stress can combine with a great conversational flexibility. This principle of alliterative verse characterises the operas of the *Ring*: subsequent operas, particularly *Die Meistersinger*, progressively abandon it. In this way *Das Rheingold* can be seen as the high-water mark of a poetic revolution which, in itself and in its consequences, marks perhaps the single most decisive aesthetic breach with pre-1849 work made by Wagner in the *Ring* dramas.

Wagner enlarged his orchestral requirements in various ways for *Das Rheingold* and for the *Ring* in general. He hoped for a string section of 64 players throughout the cycle. Eighteen pitched anvils are employed for the transition between the second and third scenes of *Rheingold*, and six harps adorn the entry of the gods into Valhalla. Above all, the Valhalla theme, first heard at the start of the second scene of *Das Rheingold*, introduces the so-called 'Wagner tubas'. These instruments, to be played by a second quartet of horn players, were intended to extend downwards the characteristically rich and weighty sound of the horn section. In Paris in 1853 Wagner had seen and heard newly-constructed brass instruments, made by Sax, and in the 1870s he asked Hans Richter to procure a set of comparable instruments, probably from Moritz of Berlin, for the *Ring* premiere in Bayreuth.

Die Walküre: *Plot*

The first act is set in the hut of the warrior Hunding. After a storm a solitary male figure enters in exhaustion and throws himself on the floor of the hut. He is found by Hunding's wife Sieglinde, who gives him drink, speaks kindly to him and gradually finds herself responding with warmth to him. In his exhaustion he is similarly aroused by her. He explains that he is wounded; his enemies have broken his weapons. Her husband arrives. Sieglinde explains the stranger's plight. Suspiciously and roughly Hunding offers a formal pledge of hospitality and demands the stranger's identity. He says that his name should be Wehwalt ('Woeful'); one day, returning from hunting with his father, he found that his home was burnt, his mother murdered and his sister carried off. He became separated from his father, and found himself increasingly at odds with warrior society. One day he went to the help of a girl forced by her family into marriage with a man she hated. He killed the family but was unable to protect the woman, who died before his eyes. Hunding, listening, realises that that family was his own, and that he is sheltering his bitterest enemy. In the morning the stranger, he proclaims, will have to fight for his life. Sieglinde secretly puts a drug into her husband's drink.

As the stranger is left alone, he recalls the promise, made by his father, that when he most needed it he would find a weapon. The firelight illuminates a spot on the trunk of the tree around which the hut is built, where the hilt of a sword buried in the tree can suddenly be seen. When Sieglinde returns she tells how, at her wedding, a stranger had thrust a sword into the tree which no one could remove. Her guest proclaims that he will

Clarence Whitehill, 1871-1932, American baritone, as Wotan in *Die Walküre*.

remove the sword and claim Sieglinde as his wife. The door of the hut flies open, revealing the moon and the spring night. As the couple declare their love for each other he accepts from her the new name Siegmund (guardian of victory), and pulls the sword from the tree. They discover that they are brother and sister and embrace passionately as the act closes.

The second act is set on a high mountain. Wotan tells his daughter Brünnhilde, the Valkyrie, to grant victory to Siegmund in the impending battle. Wotan's consort Fricka arrives and demands that Wotan abide by the laws of morality, which should grant protection to Hunding against his wife's abduction, and preclude any sympathy for the incestuous love between Siegmund and Sieglinde. Wotan explains to Fricka that Siegmund is the hero, human, independent and powerful, who alone can rescue the gods from doom. Fricka suggests that he allows Siegmund's independence to be seen, by taking from him the sword he has given him. Wotan, submitting to Fricka's arguments, promises to deny protection to Siegmund. As Brünnhilde returns, he gives way to despair and shame.

He explains to her, in an immense narration, how in gaining power over the whole world he had involved himself in treaties and contracts. He tells her of Alberich's denunciation of love, of the ring and of his surrender of it to the giants. He explains to Brünnhilde that she is his daughter by Erda, the Goddess of Earth: she and her Valkyrie sisters were raised by Wotan to gather dead heroes to the fortress of Valhalla, and thus to protect the gods against the impending assault of Alberich. The ring, also, must be regained from the giant Fafner, who has transformed himself into a dragon guarding his treasure. Wotan cannot himself attack Fafner, because of his past contract with him. He needs a hero who can act on his behalf, but independently. Siegmund had been raised by Wotan, his unknown and disguised father, as such a hero. But Wotan now sees that this project cannot be fulfilled, and calls upon Brünnhilde to protect Hunding, threatening her with extreme punishment if she disobeys.

Siegmund and Sieglinde enter. Guilty and exhausted, she begs him to abandon her. As she sleeps, Brünnhilde appears to Siegmund and tells him that she will take him to Valhalla. She speaks of the joys awaiting him there, of the father whom he will meet, and of maidens who will attend on him. But he cannot take Sieglinde with him. He immovably refuses her offer, preferring mortality with his bride. Brünnhilde, aroused to extreme emotion by his human love, promises, in defiance of her father, to protect him. Hunding's horn is heard. Siegmund and Hunding fight. Brünnhilde attempts to protect Siegmund but Wotan shatters Siegmund's sword with his spear. Hunding kills Siegmund and is in turn contemptuously killed by Wotan, who sets off in pursuit of his daughter Brünnhilde.

In the final act the Valkyrie maidens gather. Brünnhilde arrives, carrying Sieglinde with her on her horse, and begs protection from her sisters. Sieglinde, after the death of her brother, longs to die in turn. But, being told that she is pregnant and that a new hero will be born to her, she begs Brünnhilde for protection. She takes with her the fragments of Siegmund's sword as she sets off eastwards for the forest. Wotan arrives: the Valkyries in vain attempt to shield Brünnhilde from his anger. He removes her privileges as a Valkyrie; he will place her on a mountain top where she will be the property of the first man who finds her. Left alone with her father, she begs him for mercy and reminds him of his own plans and desires for Siegmund. He

is angered by the reminder, but when she urges him at least to ensure that only a hero will find her on the rock, Wotan, moved by her own heroism and by his own deepest wishes, relents. As he kisses her to sleep he grants her the protection of a ring of fire around the mountain top. Only the man who does not fear the fire will claim Brünnhilde.

Die Walküre: *Commentary*

The central scene of *Die Walküre*, frequently known as '*Todesverkundigung*', ('the announcement of death'), in which Brünnhilde offers Siegmund the joys of immortality and he refuses them in favour of his love for Sieglinde, was created entirely by Wagner. In its exaltation of human over divine values, it catches to perfection the heroic humanism adopted in many of his writings by Wagner in the late 1840s, and indicates the extent to which Siegmund is indeed the independent hero desiderated by Wotan, though not one who can ever grant Wotan the protection he supposes he needs.

In many ways the opera centres on the themes of protection and freedom. The unavailing will to protect oneself is seen in Hunding's insistence on marriage rites, and in the warrior codes where males seek to determine the disposal of females – that code from which Siegmund feels himself estranged. A similar embrace of the seeming values of protection and morality appears in Fricka's demands and Wotan's yielding to them, while a powerful instinct for emotional self-protection may be discerned through the extreme anger with which Wotan greets all the suggestions of his daughter that he should yield, not to the moral code, but to his own deepest desires.

Against such protective and self-protective instincts stand out, powerfully and often beautifully, the free independence of the love of Siegmund and Sieglinde, the deep responsive awareness of Brünnhilde for Siegmund's heroism, and, most significantly, for the future operas in the cycle, Sieglinde's willingness to survive without protection, for the sake of her unborn son. This dialectic is to some extent cut across by Brünnhilde's desire to secure Siegmund against Hunding in battle, and above all on Brünnhilde's insistence on the protection that Wotan at first denies and in the end grants her – the ring of fire.

In another sense Wotan's narration in the second act stands in the centre of *Die Walküre*, drawing together the events of *Das Rheingold*, and other events undramatised in that work, and looking forward, albeit despairingly, to future events which will amount, at least for Wotan, to the end of all things. The *Ring* cycle abounds in narrations of all kinds: in this work alone, Siegmund in Act One and Sieglinde in the same act also have their own extended stories to tell. Such narrations regularly fulfil several functions at once. They bring the audience abreast of the story; they also indicate how the characters themselves seek to weave together their fixed pasts with their possible futures. The dramatic technique of narration thus goes hand in hand with the musical technique whereby the themes of the cycle are increasingly woven together with one another, as the intentions of individual characters interconnect with, and determine one another.

Of all the works of the *Ring* cycle, *Die Walküre* has proved the most popular when performed in isolation. It contains six well-differentiated parts, including Wagner's first heroic tenor, Siegmund. Each act begins in a minor key and only the third act ends in a major key. Immense excitement is conferred upon the endings of the first two acts by an accelerating tempo and an increasingly lively orchestral texture, with string writing insistently punctuated by the heavy brass instruments, which Wagner fashioned specifically for the *Ring* cycle.

The work contains a number of units separable from their context; the so-called 'spring song' of Siegmund in the first act, the 'ride of the Valkyries', and Wotan's farewell to Brünnhilde at the end of the third act. However, the single most powerful scene, the '*Todesverkundigung*', gains its entire force from its dramatic context. The texture of the love-scene between Siegmund and Sieglinde is more sustained over a long period than anything in *Das Rheingold*, as is much of the final scene between Wotan and Brünnhilde. In these passages one can begin to sense the interweaving of *motifs* with one another which becomes a hallmark of the most mature style of Wagner's operas. But much of the second act falls into the more declamatory style, associated in *Das Rheingold* with conflict between individual characters.

The dramaturgy of the second act is not only appropriate in the context of this individual opera, but is also striking in the context of the *Ring* cycle as a whole. Wotan, in the second complete act of the trilogy, is already found foreboding the end of all things. If one were to take a view of the *Ring* as essentially Wotan's drama, this would represent a serious structural imbalance. Such an 'imbalance' in fact helps an audience to develop a more justifiable view of the *Ring* as representing a transition from a God-centred to a human-centred conception of universal history.

Tristan und Isolde: *Plot*

The first act is set on board Tristan's ship as it crosses the sea from Ireland to Cornwall, bringing the Irish princess Isolde as bride for Tristan's uncle and suzerain King Mark. Isolde angrily laments her situation, and tells her maid Brangäne to summon Tristan, predicting that he will evade her summons. He does so, though politely, while his servant Kurwenal boastfully praises Tristan's heroism and Cornish manliness.

Isolde, in a long narration, tells how Tristan, wounded in battle and under a disguised name, had come to her for healing, how she recognised him as the killer of her betrothed, Morold, and how her determination to revenge herself upon Tristan had weakened as they looked into each other's eyes. Tristan had then returned to claim her as King Mark's bride. She regrets having foregone her opportunity to kill him. Brangäne uncomprehendingly suggests that she should be grateful that Tristan has rewarded her kindness with the honour of Mark's hand, and reminds her of the love-potion bequeathed to her by her mother, with which she could, at need, compel Mark's love. As the ship nears land, Isolde once more orders Tristan into her presence, saying that she will not otherwise go ashore with him to greet Mark. She then tells Brangäne to prepare not a love-potion but a death-potion; not for Mark but for Tristan. (She does not say, what Brangäne's incomprehension invites the audience to understand, that her anger with Tristan proceeds not from his offering her to Mark, but from his failure to acknowledge his own love for her.)

When Tristan at length approaches, Isolde demands vengeance. Tristan, admitting her claims, offers her his sword. Isolde calls for the drink from Brangäne and gives him the cup. He drinks; Isolde seizes it from him and drinks also. But Brangäne, whether in terror or in belated understanding, has replaced the death-potion with a love-potion, and, as Tristan's ship arrives at the shore of Cornwall and is greeted in triumph, Tristan and Isolde despairingly and ecstatically fall into each other's arms.

The second act is set in the gardens of King Mark's castle in Cornwall. Mark and his courtiers have left to go hunting, but Tristan remains behind for an assignation with Isolde in the summer night. Brangäne warns her mistress of the likely treachery of Tristan's seeming friend Melot. Isolde pours scorn on her fears and calls for her to put out the bright torch; this is the signal for Tristan to approach. The lovers greet each other ecstatically, expressing their anger at the brightness of the day which has kept them apart, and hailing the beauty of the night which allows them to share their love. As they sing together, Brangäne keeps watch and warns them from time to time of the impending day and the return of the royal party. Suddenly King Mark and his courtiers burst in. Mark has been warned by Melot of his faithful vassal Tristan's treachery. Mark, deeply

Tristan und Isolde,
Act One; triumph and
despair as the ship
reaches Cornwall.

moved, lovingly asks Tristan for an explanation, and speaks of his own grief and suffering. Tristan can only say to his king that he and Isolde no longer belong to the world of the day. As Tristan kisses Isolde, Melot draws his sword and Tristan exposes himself to it. Deeply wounded he sinks back into the arms of his vassal Kurwenal.

The third act is set in Tristan's castle in Brittany. A shepherd plays mournfully on a pipe. Kurwenal tends Tristan's wounds; he urges the shepherd to change to a joyful tune when Isolde's ship, which is expected, appears on the horizon. Tristan revives and Kurwenal explains that he has brought him back to recover in his family home in Brittany. But Tristan feels that in his survival he has lost contact with the world of Isolde and of the night. When Kurwenal tells him that a living Isolde may arrive at any time, Tristan, in delirium, thinks he sees her ship already approaching; but as the sad shepherd's tune breaks in on his ecstasy, Tristan returns to the themes of sadness, both present and past, and sinks back in acceptance of death. Yet he revives again; and finally, as he imagines the gentle and healing arrival of Isolde, the shepherd's tune, now joyful, rings out. Reality has matched Tristan's dream-vision and Isolde comes ashore. As he waits for her, Tristan tears off the bandages from his wounds; on her arrival he dies in her arms.

A second ship arrives carrying Mark and the courtiers; they

Poster for *Tristan und Isolde*, Bayreuth 1889.

fight against Tristan's followers. Kurwenal is wounded and dies at Tristan's feet. Mark seeks to prevent the fight, for he has come to surrender Isolde to Tristan. But as he laments Isolde sings of the transfiguration of their love, and at the climax of her song dies, falling on Tristan's body, united with him in death.

Tristan und Isolde: *Commentary*

Tristan und Isolde is one of the greatest hymns to love ever created in any medium. But equally the opera presents the impossibility of love; its inability to adapt itself to any worldly society, its involvement with self-destruction, its acceptance of mutual destruction and its supreme fulfilment in that death, which equally is its annihilation. In all of these ways it expresses, ratifies and, in its own way, resolves the energies and frustrations of its composer in the middle and late 1850s.

But the greatness of the work, quite apart from these qualities, corresponds to the perfection of its structure. In each of the three acts one finds a similar progression: from an introductory social situation, presented in dialogue between a principal character and a servant; through a state of extreme tension (in Acts One and Three) within the principal character, or, in Act Two, a union of the lovers in a state at once tense and resolved; and into a sudden interruption by the external world, leading precipitously to a dramatic resolution, involving both love and death.

In the first act Isolde's tension between her familial loyalty and her feelings for Tristan, at first partly unrealised, and until the end of the act largely unexpressed, forms the musical and dramatic centre. In the last act, Tristan's physical suffering is transmuted into the tension between his desire to see Isolde once more in the flesh and his increasingly powerful commitment of himself to death. In the second act the lovers join together in a forty-minute love-duet through which they express, separately and together, both their physical union and their acceptance of the gulf this union sets between them and any of the terms of human society upon which that union could find conventional ratification.

This sense of a logical contradiction between love and society is, for narrative purposes, embedded in a world of medieval codes of honour. These put Tristan, loving his master's intended bride, into an impossible position, and mark him and, to a certain extent, Isolde also, with the stigma of treachery. This theme is sustained in the presentation of the several minor characters, all bound by ties of feudal duty to their social superiors. And *Tristan*, which is so central in Wagner's work for

Tristan und Isolde at Covent Garden, London.

its presentation of a love which annihilates individual and social identity alike, thus also takes its stand alongside *Rienzi, Lohengrin* and, in certain ways, *Götterdämmerung* and *Die Meistersinger* as a presentation of the pressures of social bonds upon individual energies and their fulfilment.

In most important ways the verbal and musical style of the work are remarkably different from those of the works of the *Ring*, whose composition it interrupted. Much of the verse is rhymed; there is frequent juxtaposition of words with similar sounds; there is a fair amount of word-play, and in any case the music, in its power, its volume, frequently so dominates the voices as to render the individual words inaudible. There is, alongside many powerful extended solo passages, a significant amount of writing for voices in duet.

Above all the harmonic language of the work marks a leap beyond the norms, not only of Wagner's own style hitherto, but of virtually all the accepted canons of nineteenth-century writing. Wagner would have been able to study recent orchestral work by Liszt, and been aware of the potential extensions of key-relations implicit in the late work of Beethoven. But the harmonic practice of *Tristan und Isolde*, beyond anything in the practice of these composers, goes a long way towards the establishment of dissonant chords as a harmonic norm. The listener is thus acclimatised to a sustained degree of harmonic tension, corresponding to the emotional tension which (the drama suggests) is involved precisely in the most fulfilling and shared of human loves. The first chord heard in the prelude would allow analysis in terms of any one of eight different keys, and could lead into any one of the other sixteen remaining possible keys within the major-minor system. Thus from the start the work points towards the possible future supersession of this 'diatonic' key-system, by the language of 'atonality', eventually developed, in different emotional contexts and with far more parade of theoretical deliberation, by Schoenberg and his pupils in the second and third decades of the twentieth century.

The language of *Tristan und Isolde* frequently sets passages of regular, usually major-key, writing alongside the heavily dissonant, restless and chromatic musical language given to the lovers. Thus the antithesis, of consciousness and of social being, between the lovers and their world is given graphic and immediate expression; never more so than in the stunning climax to the first act, when the revelation of Tristan and Isolde's love coincides with their arrival in the social world of the Cornish kingdom which will destroy it.

Chapter 6

Favourite and Victor

In 1864 Wagner's life became transformed. Gifts and financial support from the new King of Bavaria, Ludwig II, put his finances on as firm a footing as they were ever to be in his lifetime. The love of Cosima, Liszt's illegitimate daughter and the wife of Hans von Bülow, was to renew Wagner's emotional life, to give him three children, all born out of marriage, and to lead to his second marriage in 1870. In 1869 the first portions of the *Ring* to be seen were premiered in Munich at the will of Ludwig, though very much against the will of Wagner. Later in 1869 Wagner resumed composition on the *Ring* with the third act of *Siegfried*. By 1874 the score of *Götterdämmerung* and thus of the whole four-part work was complete. The cycle was given three complete performances in 1876 in an entirely new theatre built at Wagner's direction. The performers, both vocal and orchestral, were recruited, trained and largely directed by him. 1876 marks thus the climax of twelve years of personal success and creative fulfilment for Wagner.

Yet in some ways the Wagner of these twelve years emerges as a less sympathetic figure than the youth and middle-aged man, who were driven by emotional needs and financial precariousness. The beneficence of Ludwig involved Wagner in political intrigues at Ludwig's court, from which he was not wise enough to abstain, and Ludwig's determination to control the performances of works for which, in effect, he had already paid Wagner handsomely, was to lead to frequent rifts between the two men. Ludwig was also the victim of systematic deceit by Wagner and by Cosima, who for a long time concealed from him the nature of their relationship (partly to secure the position of Cosima's husband Hans, for whom Wagner had obtained employment at Ludwig's court).

Wagner's relationship with Cosima had to face the problems caused by her infidelity to her husband and by the malice to which this exposed him. Subsequently more difficulties were caused by Cosima's Catholicism (an obstacle to divorce) and by the inevitable hostility of Liszt, Cosima's father and himself a Catholic in minor priestly orders. In all these vicissitudes the determination of Cosima and of Ludwig, in their different ways, upon securing their own personal stakes in Wagner stands out more clearly than any initiatives taken towards either by Wagner himself. His life over these twelve years was taken up largely with musical composition and with plans for building his own homes, and eventually his own festival theatre. It is as if the new directions taken by his life, over these ostensibly successful years, happened through him rather than being led by him. Certainly he welcomed the freedom for musical creativity allowed to him by the intense and passionate initiatives taken by Ludwig and Cosima on his behalf.

There is more to be said. In these years Wagner was becoming a great man. Visitors from Germany and France came to his homes, to discuss music, poetry, drama and philosophy and simply to encounter the man and take away a unique sense of artistic greatness. Wagner lent himself, sometimes graciously, sometimes bombastically, to this process of canonization. Some of the prose writings from this period remain, like those of the late 1840s and the early 1850s, essentially practical in their emphasis, however contorted in their processes of argumentation; but in others, Wagner gives full scope to his penchant for generalised, and frequently viciously destructive, polemic against rivals, enemies and whole nations and cultural traditions.

Ludwig of Bavaria

Ludwig came to the throne of Bavaria on March 10th 1864 when he was eighteen years old. Bavaria was one of the largest of the kingdoms, originally within the Holy Roman Empire, which retained different degrees of genuine external as well as internal political self-determination. Ludwig's position gave him considerable potential importance in the complex politics of central Europe over the next seven years. But his own concerns were overwhelmingly with art, architecture, drama and music. Wagner's work was known to him: in his fantasies he had already inserted himself as a Wagnerian protagonist in an imagined heroic life. His ideal self-image was that of Lohengrin, knight of the swan and servant of the grail. Wagner and his music dramas represented for Ludwig this grail.

His first act as king was to send his cabinet secretary to Wagner (who postponed seeing the man, supposing that it was yet another of his creditors) to summon him for a first audience of one-and-a-half hours. Wagner's creditors were to be paid off: Wagner was installed at a house, Villa Pellet, near the King's own castle, Schloss Berg, on the shores of the lake Starnberg near Munich. While the king was in the castle he and Wagner

King Ludwig II of Bavaria, 1845-1886; Wagner's patron, declared insane and deposed three years after Wagner's death.

met more days than not. In October the king arranged for Wagner to take over a large house in Munich, and provided for a regular annual salary, together with considerable removal expenses. In return for this he requested, and was given, the copyright of the *Ring*.

Wagner's enjoyment of luxurious furniture and clothing, already seen under conditions of debt in Vienna the previous

year, was now free to emerge in its full glory. And, though the
completion of the *Ring*, which was the discharge of Ludwig's
reward, was likely to take a number of years, there was a
recompense nearer at hand for Ludwig to enjoy. *Tristan und
Isolde*, completed in 1861, still awaited a première, though
Wagner had already begun training the singers, a husband and
wife pair, Ludwig and Malvina Schnorr von Carolsfeld, who
were to take the two leading roles. On June 10th 1865 *Tristan
und Isolde* received its première. The audience was thus enabled
to hear Wagner's first complete performed music drama since
Lohengrin seventeen years earlier. The conductor of the premiere
was Hans von Bülow.

Cosima von Bülow
It is hard to estimate the responses either of Hans or of Cosima,
still officially his wife, to the music-drama of passionate

Hans von Bülow, 1830-1894; conductor, composer and pianist, he conducted the first performances of *Tristan und Isolde* and *Die Meistersinger*. His wife Cosima became Wagner's second wife.

adulterous love, which Wagner had conceived in the context of an earlier love affair. Cosima's physical relationship with Wagner had been consummated in June 1864 when she spent some days with him at Starnberg in advance of her husband's arrival. She became pregnant, and in April 1865 gave birth to her first daughter by Wagner, Isolde. Isolde's true parentage was not acknowledged: Cosima remained in the eyes of the world Hans's wife. Wagner's enemies at the court of Ludwig were already hinting, and more, at the true situation. Wagner and Cosima were led into elaborate deceptions in order to conceal the truth from Ludwig. The deceptions continued for at least a year after Isolde's birth.

Cosima and Wagner had declared their love for each other in Vienna late in 1863 ('with sobs and tears' as Wagner was to write in his autobiography). Cosima's tears may have registered a sense of triumph. She had won the heart, as she was later to win the hand, of a composer in whose greatness she totally believed and whom she saw it as her mission to vindicate in the eyes of the world. For Wagner, Cosima no doubt represented youth, conceivably beauty and certainly an important artistic connection with Franz Liszt. She may also have represented a social cultivation and self-confidence which Wagner's early life had not given him. It is possible to feel that, for Cosima, Wagner became a possession; and that, through a mixture of passivity and calculation, he allowed himself to become her possession in all ways other than musical and artistic. But he had profound emotional reasons for gratitude to her. She gave him the children he had never had. She presided over a financial and domestic stability, even, in a paradoxical way, a propriety which he had only enjoyed for rare periods in his earlier life.

He may have reflected that he gained these crucial gifts at the price of his own subsequent sexual and emotional freedom. He had had affairs, emotional and physical, before Cosima and he was to do so, or to wish to do so, again, but Cosima was to prove vigilant in guarding her possession. The tension between freedom and constraints, which Wagner's marriage involved for him, emerged most forcefully in his last years. It may have led directly to his death.

Ludwig and Wagner formed splendid plans for the performance of Wagner's dramatic works in Munich. The architect Gottfried Semper was summoned in autumn 1864, to design a festival theatre suitable for the eventual performance of the *Ring*. Plans were laid down for the establishment of a music school, under the direction of Hans von Bülow, who was appointed the court Kapellmeister in 1867. In December 1867, Hans Richter, subsequently the first director of the complete *Ring* cycle at Bayreuth, was appointed repetiteur at the court theatre.

The expenses involved in these plans, coupled with the even greater expenses involved in Ludwig's far more fantastic architectural projects, mobilised powerful forces in Bavarian politics. The king's own wishes in architecture were difficult to attack directly. Wagner offered a more exposed target. Opposition focused on Wagner's personal life. Malvina Schnorr, the first singer of Isolde, was particularly virulent in denouncing the actual, though concealed, relationship between Wagner and Cosima. At the end of 1865 Ludwig, much against his will, was forced to banish Wagner from Bavaria.

In March 1866 Cosima joined Wagner in Geneva. They made a home for themselves in the house Tribschen, situated on Lake Lucerne. There in May Ludwig visited them on his birthday,

Tribschen, on Lake Lucerne, home of Wagner and Cosima from 1866 to 1872.

announcing himself as Walther von Stolzing, the name of the hero in Wagner's *Die Meistersinger*, then in process of composition.

The politics of central Europe became volatile in 1866. In June the Prussian army invaded Austria. Wagner advised Ludwig to remain independent between the two warring parties. Ludwig sided with Austria, whose army, to the surprise of the rest of Europe, was overwhelmingly defeated by the Prussian forces on July 3rd at the battle of Königgrätz. Wagner's advice, prudent as it was, indicated the extent to which his political energies of the late 1840s and the early 1850s had metamorphosed. In the years after 1866 Wagner, largely against the current of feeling in the Bavarian court, discovered in himself, like other liberal German intellectuals, a growing enthusiasm for German national unity under the banner of the King of Prussia. Despite the Bavarian defeat, Ludwig regained popularity with his subjects by engagement to his cousin. At the end of 1866 Wagner's enemies at the Bavarian court were expelled in their turn.

Wagner's and Cosima's second child, Eva, was born in February 1867, to be followed by Siegfried, Wagner's only son, born in June 1869. By this time Wagner had completed *Die*

Meistersinger, and in June 1868 Bülow conducted its première at the Munich court theatre. After two successful major premières, the theatre seemed to Ludwig more than adequate to handle the component parts of the *Ring* as and when they were completed. In early 1869 Wagner had to deal with Ludwig's inevitable demand for the première of *Das Rheingold* to be given in Munich. Wagner was hostile to any attempt at performance of the parts of the *Ring* in isolation from one another. This typical instinct against separation and in favour of continuity would have been given a new spur by his resumption of work on *Siegfried* in March of that year.

But *Das Rheingold* was premièred in 1869 and *Die Walküre* followed it in June 1870. Both works were well received, and the subsequent achievement of the complete cycle in its Bayreuth incarnation certainly owed much to the pioneering work of the Munich performers. It is hard to believe that Wagner would have had even such success as he did achieve, with great difficulty, in engaging singers and instrumentalists for the Bayreuth performances, had he not been able to point to the Munich performances as proof of the potential stageworthiness of such elaborate works.

After the birth of Eva Wagner, the liaison between Wagner and Cosima could scarcely be misunderstood. In November 1868 Cosima finally moved in to the Tribschen house with her two daughters, and Ludwig was officially informed of the true nature of their relationship. Cosima remained hesitant about divorce from Bülow; it would embarrass her father Liszt, now in minor Catholic orders, as would, even more, any subsequent Protestant marriage to Wagner.

In August of that year Wagner had begun sketches for a dramatic work entitled *Luthers Hochzeit* ('Luther's Wedding'), which stressed Luther's Protestant teaching concerning the positive value of marriage. 1868 was being celebrated as the 350th anniversary of the Reformation; Sachs's ode in praise of Luther, 'the Wittenberg nightingale', is movingly sung by the people of Nuremberg in the final scene of *Die Meistersinger*. Thus the opera points indirectly towards the resolution of emotional and familial tensions that Wagner desired; marriage with Cosima, following her divorce and her adoption of the Lutheran faith, and followed by the upbringing of their children as Protestants. Wagner was seeking to make his life as unified and as comfortable as possible.

Friends and foes

It is ironic that in the same late months of 1868 Wagner met, on a visit to Leipzig, the philosopher who, though at first one of his most passionate devotees, was to prove subsequently the most

Culture and domesticity; Wagner at home with Cosima and (by the window) his father-in-law, Liszt.

hostile of his critics, and whose criticism was to focus on precisely these targets: unity, comfort and consolation. Friedrich Nietzsche, born in 1844, was one of a number of admirers from a younger generation to visit Wagner in Tribschen in 1869. Others included the French poet Villiers de l'Isle Adam, Catulle Mendès and his wife Judith Gautier-Mendès, later Wagner's close friend and perhaps lover. It is piquant to note the admiration of these and other French artists for Wagner in the years in which Franco-German tension was moving towards outright political hostility. French visitors at Tribschen, on the very day war was declared between France and Prussia, included the composers Saint-Saens and Duparc. Wagner was provoked during their visit into direct insults towards their nationality and culture.

The Prussian army defeated the French forces in 1870 with the same speed and almost insulting ease as it had the Austrians four years earlier. Wagner hailed the victory in November of that year by writing a farce, *A Capitulation*. Its title bore reference to the French military capitulation to Germany: but its theme, though expressed ironically, was the past capitulation of German national culture to France. 1870, like some earlier years, saw Wagner's life and German politics moving in pace with each other. While Germany emerged as indisputably the foremost power in Central Europe, and while the Prussian kingdom, assuming control of all German forces, prepared for its change into the second German Empire, so Cosima's marriage with Hans was dissolved and the ground was left clear for her marriage to Wagner in the Protestant church in Lucerne on August 25th. The *Siegfried Idyll* was composed by Wagner for Christmas Day of that year; it honoured Cosima's birthday and the name and imagined future of their son Siegfried. Its performance on the staircase of the Wagners' house at Tribschen signalled their domestic fulfilment.

The composition of the opera *Siegfried* was completed shortly afterwards, in early February 1871. Wagner had already begun the music for the text of what now became *Götterdämmerung*, the drama which he had conceived as early as 1848, under the title of *Siegfrieds Tod*. The draft score was complete by 1872. The full score of *Götterdämmerung*, and thus of the whole *Ring* cycle, was completed on November 24th 1874.

Bayreuth

Well before this time plans were advanced for the performance of the complete cycle – not, as Ludwig had wished, in Munich, but in the small town of Bayreuth in northern Bavaria. Bayreuth, situated at almost the exact centre of Germany as it was now constituted, was a predominantly Protestant enclave within Catholic Bavaria, with an impressive legacy of buildings from the era of Wilhelmine, the favourite sister of Frederick the Great, and wife of the Margrave Frederick. These historical links with Prussia suited the pro-Bismarckian mood of Wagner in the 1870s; on the other hand, he still needed Ludwig's patronage, and therefore a home in Bavaria. He wanted his home to be where his theatre was; and for the theatre he was set against large cities and summer resorts, with the audiences that they implied. The existing theatre at Bayreuth was reputed to have the largest stage in Europe, but, after casting their eyes over it in April 1871, the Wagners conceived the idea of constructing an entirely new theatre.

Wagner acquired a site by the Palace Gardens in Bayreuth for his future family home, which was known as Wahnfried, a name that might be translated 'Peace in Illusion'. In Wagner's original conception the money for the building in Bayreuth was to be raised by Wagner societies and by private patrons, as well as through the support of the Bayreuth town council. Since Ludwig held the copyright of the *Ring*, his acceptance of this plan was crucial, and, though Wagner's plans ran directly against Ludwig's private wishes, the acceptance was granted. In May 1872 the foundations of the Bayreuth theatre were laid. Ludwig was absent, but sent his good wishes.

While building proceeded for the theatre, not only the completed composition but also the singers were lacking. Throughout 1872 and 1873 Wagner toured German opera houses far and wide in search of singers. He also conducted

sequences of concerts to raise funds, in 1873 and more continu-
ously in 1875. These concert tours took him as far afield as
Vienna, Budapest and Berlin. By the end of 1873 lack of funds
was endangering the whole project and Wagner was driven to
ask Ludwig for help, which late in January 1874 he provided,
though only in the form of a loan. This involved the prices for
tickets being set at a level which precluded Wagner's earlier
hopes for a wide, and genuinely democratic, audience for his
national epic cycle, and which set the pattern for the subsequent
financial levels of the Bayreuth audience.

Rehearsals for the cycle, with such singers as by now had
been engaged, began as early as the summer of 1874, under the
direction of Hans Richter. They were resumed in the summer of
the following year. By then it had become apparent that no
performance of the cycle would be possible until 1876. Wagner
had thus spent much of the first half of the 1870s involved in
the practicalities of performance, and his energies were given
tirelessly to the coaching of the singers in 1875 and again in
1876. He also took a substantial part in the direction of
movement and gesture. This was a new field of creativity for
him and one in which he left the performers significantly more
freedom, both for their own considered contributions and for
improvisations in the course of the performance, than was later
to become the custom at Bayreuth under the direction of Cosima
after Wagner's death.

The *Ring* cycle

The improvisatory nature of Wagner's own skills, and the
artistic self-confidence which allowed him to shift his energies
from one field to another of dramatic creativity, were never
more apparent than at this remarkably late stage of his career.
He might have preferred to conduct the cycle himself, since he
demonstrated dissatisfaction with the tempi chosen by Hans
Richter. But the success achieved by the three cycles, given from
August 13th 1876 onwards, was such as to set all these
criticisms and reservations in the background. The audiences at
these *Ring* cycles included the composers Bruckner,
Tchaikovsky, Grieg and Saint-Saens, and the crowned heads,
Ludwig of Bavaria, Wilhelm I Emperor of all Germany, and
Pedro II of Brazil. Nietzsche, who had been a regular visitor
both at Tribschen and at Wahnfried until 1874, also attended
the cycle, but left before the end of it, suffering from illness,
certainly physical but also perhaps psychological. 1876 marked
Wagner's greatest musical triumphs – and also the emergence of
the breach between him and his most enthusiastic philosophical
and cultural supporter.

These years also saw Wagner's return to prose writing.

**Ground plan of the
theatre at Bayreuth, with
inset sectional view.**

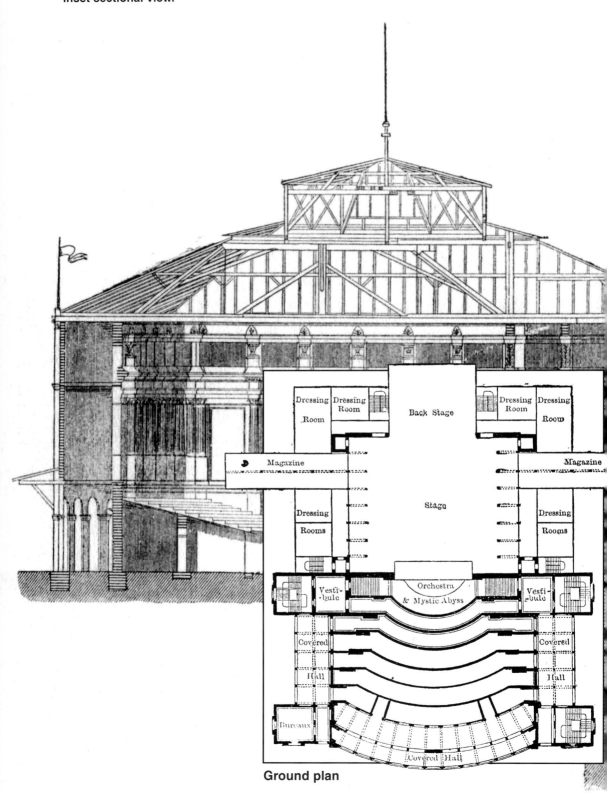

Ground plan

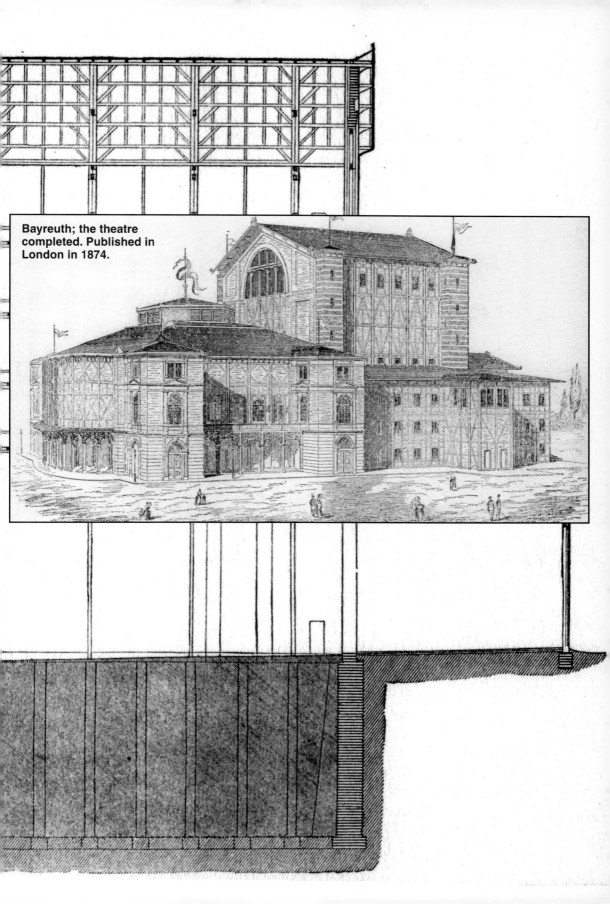

Bayreuth; the theatre completed. Published in London in 1874.

Luther's Wedding of 1868 was followed in 1869 by a reprint of the earlier pamphlet 'Jewishness in Music', with a new prologue voicing complaints at Wagner's supposed persecution by cabals of Jewish artists – complaints particularly scurrilous and misdirected when one considers the immense personal support, at sacrificial levels of devotion, Wagner received in these years and until the end of his life from Jewish conductors at Bayreuth. The farce *A Capitulation* of November 1870 was accompanied in the same year by an essay 'Beethoven', in celebration of that composer's centenary, in which Wagner sought to bring into line with each other his earlier work in opera and drama, and his subsequent commitment to the teachings of Schopenhauer. In 'Beethoven' music is envisaged as the ultimate vehicle of musical theatre, but Wagner stresses that the fusion of music and words confers more power on the artistic object than either music or words could achieve in isolation.

Wagner would have needed some such compromise, not only with his earlier written works, but also between their emphases and the actual complex and variegated aesthetic implied by the *Ring* cycle itself, in order to feel at ease with his theoretical conscience. A similar sense of stock-taking appears in the foreword which Wagner wrote in 1871 for the projected publication of his collected writings. These emerged in nine volumes between 1871 and 1873. A text entitled 'On Actors and Singers' (1872) indicated the practical demands, and the aesthetic justification of these demands, posed by the impending completion of the *Ring*.

In 1876 Wagner could well have considered his artistic mission discharged and his career completed. He was certainly also well into the business of regarding his career as one more artistic artefact. One of the earliest marks of Cosima's influence over him had been his autobiography, *My Life*, which he began writing in 1865, and for which he was to prepare a carefully edited version of his pre-Cosima life. This autobiography has conferred on much subsequent Wagner criticism and scholarship the frequently misleading impression of a career lived from start to finish in full historical consciousness of creative purpose and with a total commitment to unflinching self-expression. But the triumph of 1876 owed as much to Wagner's genius for improvisation, and to his still remarkable physical stamina, as to any undivided historical or creative will. It owed perhaps even more to his two protectors, patrons and – he may often have felt – friendly enemies, Ludwig and Cosima.

Chapter 7

Music Dramas: 1861-1874

Die Meistersinger von Nüremberg: *Plot*

The opera is set in the free city of Nüremberg in the early part of
the sixteenth century. The first act opens inside the church of St
Catherine. At the end of a hymn (to St John the Baptist) the
young knight Walther von Stolzing attempts to introduce himself
to the young woman Eva. She is the daughter of his host,
Pogner, a goldsmith and a leading member of the guild of mastersingers. Walther wants to know whether she is engaged to be
married. Her maid Magdalena tells him that she will marry the
man, as yet unidentified, who wins a song contest to be held the
next day, mid-summer's day (St John's Day). Walther seeks to
enter the contest, and is told that he must learn the rules of the
mastersingers to have any chance of victory. Magdalena tells her
friend David, apprentice to the shoesmith Hans Sachs, to
instruct Walther. At great and pedantic length David goes
through the list of 'tones' to be learnt by any candidate for the
guild; Walther is overwhelmed.

As the apprentices set up a stage for the impending meeting of
the mastersingers, Walther leaves and Pogner enters, with
another of the mastersingers, the town clerk, Beckmesser.
Beckmesser has high hopes of marrying Eva and is insinuating
himself in her father's favour. Pogner assures Beckmesser of his
friendship, but equally welcomes Walther, with surprise, to the
meeting. The mastersingers assemble and their names are read
out by Köthner, the baker. Pogner explains that he wishes to
present a prize in the next day's public song contest; as a sign of
the seriousness of his commitment, and the commitment of the
German bourgeoisie, to musical culture, this prize will be the
thing he loves most: his only daughter, Eva. He includes a
proviso that she herself must love the victor. Sachs, perhaps
ironically, argues that this proviso is unlikely to tally with the
terms of the competition, and suggests that the people
themselves should be the judges. His proposal is dismissed.

Walther is introduced by Pogner, and greeted with subversive scepticism by Beckmesser, who sees him as an aristocratic upstart, and a potential rival for Eva. Walther tells how he has learnt a love of poetry and music from his reading in the culture of old German poetry. Beckmesser, the 'marker' to the mastersingers, takes his stand and Köthner reads the rules for any new song. Walther sings of spring and of the life and love which it inspires. Beckmesser's chalk scratches on his slate as he marks the faults of Walther's song. But Sachs admires Walther's originality and points to the highly partial judgement passed by Beckmesser, rival as he is for Eva's hand. Sachs urges Walther to complete the song, but Beckmesser leads the other masters in a mounting chorus of disapproval. Finally Walther strides from the church; Sachs, gazing at the slate covered with Beckmesser's marks, ponders on the beauty of Walther's song.

The second act is set in a street where we see the houses of Pogner and Sachs. It is evening. Magdalena asks David how Walther had fared, and blames him for his failure. Pogner slowly and belatedly realises Eva's affection for the young knight. Sachs, working alone on a bench outside his workshop, meditates on the beauty of the evening, and its resonance with the song he heard in the church. Eva tries to elicit from him the likely result of the next day's contest; as she flirts with him, she is drawn into a direct admission of her love for Walther. Magdalena warns her that her father is calling for her and that Beckmesser plans to serenade her; but she waits long enough for Walther to arrive. They consider elopement. Eva changes clothes with Magdalena; the lovers are about to escape when Sachs allows his lamp to illuminate the street. They hide, as Beckmesser tunes his lute ready to serenade Eva. Sachs obstructs the serenade with his own cobbling song. Beckmesser angrily implores him to be silent. Sachs suggests that they can both fulfil their aims if he hammers while marking thus any technical faults committed by Beckmesser in his serenade. Beckmesser sings and Sachs finds fault; the developing commotion calls David and the rest of the people out on to the streets in a riot, during which Beckmesser is soundly beaten by David, who imagines it was Magdalena whom he was serenading. The night-watchman's horn drives the crowd off the streets.

The first scene of the third act is set in Sachs's workshop. David enters, and Sachs breaks his meditation by ordering David to sing the song he has prepared. David sings in honour of St John and is praised by Sachs. Left alone, Sachs sings of the folly and vanity of human affairs. He considers how, with care, wisdom and trickery, he can convert this vanity into a fruitful resolution of the several crises of the work, as night is turned to day.

Walther, entering, tells Sachs of a dream he has had that night – wonderful but not to be represented in everyday language, nor in the overt canons of traditional art. Sachs explains the necessity of doing so, and justifies those canons which Walther has hitherto heard expounded only as abstract demands. Under Sachs's guidance, Walther begins to develop the words and music of what will become his 'prize song'.

After he leaves with Sachs, Beckmesser enters and picks up the song which Sachs has taken down from Walther's dictation. Imagining that it indicates Sachs's intention of competing in the contest, he challenges Sachs on his return. He is first dismayed, and then grossly delighted, when Sachs makes him a present of the composition. He leaves to memorise the song. Eva enters, pretending to complain about the shoes that Sachs has made for her. She still hopes Sachs may resolve her anxieties. When Walther arrives, the love between Walther and Eva becomes unmistakable. Sachs, though at first irritated by the mutual absorption of the lovers, eventually calls upon Walther to sing the culminating verse of his song. As he does so, Eva bursts out,

Emil Fischer, a leading Wagner baritone of the 1890s, as Hans Sachs in *Die Meistersinger*.

avowing both her love for Walther and what could have been her love for Sachs. Sachs reminds her of the story of Tristan and Isolde, and of the damaging jealousy in which any expression of his own feelings would involve all three of them. As Magdalena and David arrive, dressed for the great day, Sachs promotes his apprentice to a 'journeyman', and the five characters join in, as Sachs puts it, baptizing Walter's new song.

The scene changes to an open meadow on the river Pegnitz. The various guilds arrive in procession, each with their own songs; the apprentices join with girls in a dance. The people hail the masters, as they enter in procession, and sing a hymn (its words written by the historical Hans Sachs, in honour of Martin Luther). Sachs acknowledges their praise and explains to the people the terms of the coming contest. Beckmesser sings first, with Köthner as marker; he has totally failed both to memorise the song's words and to understand the relation between them and the music they require; his own tune involves grotesque mis-understandings of both rhythm and sense. He runs away as the crowd mock him.

Sachs explains that when truly understood, and given its appropriate music, the song deserves the people's approval; he calls upon Walther to give it its proper performance. Walther sings and is awarded the prize. Pogner invites him to join the guild of mastersingers. After his initial refusal (he claims Eva is all that he needs) he is persuaded by Sachs's explanation of the importance of the masters' traditions and of the cultural continuity which they represent for the German people. The chorus concludes the work with praise for Hans Sachs and for 'Holy German Art'.

Die Meistersinger: *Commentary*

In this work, Wagner sets forth the most congenial resolution available, in his entire output, of an endemic tension – between the demands of traditional musico-dramatic language, and the pressure of new individual creative energies of which Wagner's own work, up to this date, has provided the most striking example. Walther can only win Eva by accepting Pogner as his father-in-law, and accepting the claims upon his art of conventional verbal and musical language and structure. Such traditional language is embodied in *Die Meistersinger* in a prevalence of verbal rhyme and of musical counterpoint, the most traditional of German musical arts, associated with J.S. Bach and his seventeenth- and sixteenth-century German precursors.

The work's harmonic language, equally, strikingly contrasts with *Tristan und Isolde*, and also with those parts of the *Ring*

Poster for 1889
Bayreuth production
of *Die Meistersinger*.

Die Meistersinger at
Covent Garden in
1990; Reiner
Goldberg, as Walther,
baffles the assembled
Masters (Act One
finale).

composed later. Major keys overwhelmingly predominate; the
harmonic tensions and the high level of dissonance of *Tristan
und Isolde* are almost entirely absent. The work abounds in
choruses; the third-act quintet forms a musical and emotional
climax; set pieces can be, and frequently are, extracted from the
continuous flow of music. The use of hymns indicates Wagner's
willingness to cast his sense of German musical and dramatic
tradition into the shapes of religious as of symphonic art.

In its drama, as in its musical style, *Die Meistersinger* avoids
the starkly antithetical presentation of love and society which
dominates *Tristan und Isolde*, presenting instead, in apparently
limitless detail, a living community, within whose interactions
there is room for both intense individual energies and accepted
family bonds. But the inclusiveness has its limits, and these
limits are most obviously marked out by the treatment given to
Beckmesser. He is presented almost entirely as a figure of spite,
envy and self-serving blindness; his fate, condemned by
unanimous public mockery, is the harshest meted out to any of
Wagner's characters. One may interestingly contrast the
forgiveness granted to the wicked viceroy Friedrich (in *Das
Liebesverbot*) by the generous populace. Some productions of
Die Meistersinger seek to restore Beckmesser to the community,
bringing him back on the stage at the end. The absence of any
such direction in Wagner's text indicates the specificity and
difficulty of the apparent resolution which *Die Meistersinger*
offers.

At this ending of the opera the German and, to that extent, exclusive nature of Wagner's imagined social and artistic community is most prominent. It is not simply that the work embodies a genuinely German (rather than Italian or French) operatic and musical tradition. This tradition, in the words of Sachs's final monologue, defines itself by its fear of, and its wish to exclude, foreign (most emphatically French) traditions – an indication of the limited, and in many ways fearful, nature of Wagner's art even at its most apparently expansive.

The work thus takes to a culmination a tendency, common in Wagner, to conceal one set of themes beneath the guise of another. But whereas in earlier works Wagner had offered an ostensible set of conflicts as the story-line, through which a more sensitive exploration of contradictions within individuals and society could be explored, in *Die Meistersinger* the process is somewhat reversed. A story relying on the notion of resolvable conflict gives rise, in its conclusion, to a resolution beyond which far more intense conflicts, social and historical, may be expected.

This must seem an ungrateful reading of that opera of Wagner's perhaps most enjoyed by the largest number of listeners. Successful performances do indeed have the power to invigorate and assimilate audiences; rather as Sachs seeks to reconcile the demands of high musical culture with the criteria of democratic approval. But the opera places strain on its audiences by its extreme length. Again, it is in the third act that this length swells to gargantuan proportions; it is as long as the first two put together, and it contains four of Sachs's five monologues. The centrality of Sachs as mediator in this act supervenes over the succinctly-presented conflicts between other characters. What the work may thus seem to gain in philosophical reach, through Sachs's meditations on the relation between illusion and creative potential in human affairs, it could also be felt to lose, in terms of earlier flexibility of musical language and, particularly in Act Two, dramatic movement. Of the work's last forty-five minutes, only Beckmesser's final, and derided, song contains much music not already heard extensively before. One possible reaction to this, though scarcely expected or wished by Wagner, would be to enjoy precisely those ungainly and disconcerting features of Beckmesser's song which, by their archaism, mark a refreshing difference from the perhaps over-mature harmonic richness of their context.

The work was completed at a time when the stability of German cultural and political institutions had become of great value and necessity for Wagner. The success of the Prussians against Austria was pointing the hopes even of German liberals towards an impending unification of all Germany, under the

banner of the Prussian army and the rule of the Prussian King
Wilhelm and his chancellor Bismarck. It is interesting that *Die
Meistersinger* avoids any panegyric for kings, emperors or high
statesmen, devoting itself instead to the celebration of a
Germanic free city and, within it, to a self-regulating guild.

By now it was both safe and congenial for Wagner to imagine
himself in Walther as a partial outsider, whose charm and youth
carry all before them. On his travels, in the 1830s and 1840s,
Wagner had been, in his own eyes, much more in the position of
the outcast: the Beckmesser, whose innovations and, equally,
attempts at adaptation to the prevailing culture, were greeted
alike with uncomprehending hostility. The dramatic rejection of
Beckmesser by the citizens of Nüremberg involved for Wagner a
rehearsal, under a safe disguise, of a kind of self-punishment not
alien to his character or his circumstances in the 1840s and
1850s. But the exclusion of Beckmesser invites comparison also
with other exclusions, those of Alberich and Mime in the *Ring*,
and of Klingsor in *Parsifal* – characters for whom no space,
emotional or dramatic, can be found in such resolutions as those
dramas offer.

Recent arguments, based on the physiological as well as the
musical language used by Wagner to depict Beckmesser, have
lent weight to a view that anti-Semitic stereotypes were deployed
in this role, in ways Wagner could have expected to be recognisable. If so, then their effect, magnified by the comic and
'generous' guise under which the work has regularly been
accepted, amounts to one of the most dangerous and profoundly
objectionable features in all Wagner's work. It is impossible to
watch *Die Meistersinger*, in our time, with innocent eyes; and,
though it is possible to listen to the music with innocent, and for

much of the time with grateful and rewarded ears, the long course of the third act, through repetitions amounting eventually to a virtual harmonic and thematic standstill, may suggest a musical imagination pushing itself wilfully near the limits of its inventive powers.

Siegfried: *Plot*

The first act is set in a cave amongst rocks in the forest. The cave is inhabited by the young hero Siegfried, who has been tended through childhood by the dwarf Mime. Mime is hammering at an anvil, seeking to forge a sword for Siegfried, but in vain. He possesses the fragments of Siegmund's sword, but cannot forge them. If that sword were forged, Siegfried could kill the dragon, Fafner, with it, and Mime could gain from Siegfried the ring guarded by Fafner. Siegfried arrives and scornfully destroys Mime's latest attempt at a sword. He demands the true story of his parentage. Mime, after ineffectually claiming to be the boy's father, tells of Siegfried's mother, whom he had once found in a cave. She died in childbirth. As proof Mime shows Siegfried the fragments of his father's sword. Siegfried orders Mime to forge them, and departs for the forest.

Wotan appears disguised as a wanderer. He challenges Mime to a contest of questions. Mime asks him the names of the races that live under the earth, upon the earth and amongst the clouds: Wotan correctly answers him – the Nibelungs, the giants and the Gods. Wotan in turn asks the names of the people most loved, but most harshly treated by Wotan; of the sword to be wielded by Siegfried; and of the one who will forge the sword. To this last question Mime has no answer; the wanderer tells him that it will be one who knows no fear. He will also, says the wanderer, claim Mime's head.

Mime is torn between the need for the ring, which can be gained only by the fearlessness of Siegfried, and his own need to protect himself from Siegfried by teaching the boy fear. Siegfried, returning, scorns Mime's attempts to terrify him. He seizes the fragments of the sword, and, seeing that Mime cannot and will not forge them, sets about the task himself. As he sings over his work, Mime plans to give him a poisoned drink after he has won the ring, gaining the ring for himself and protecting himself from the conquering hero. The sword is successfully forged; Siegfried strikes the anvil and splits it in two.

As the second act begins, Alberich watches Fafner's cave in the forest. He is engaged in conversation by Wotan. He mocks Wotan with a reminder of his own ambitions. Wotan, now resigned and philosophical, warns Alberich of his vulnerability to Siegfried. Alberich retires, as Mime and Siegfried arrive.

Mime tells Siegfried what he should fear from the dragon.
Siegfried, entirely unalarmed, dismisses Mime. Left alone, for
the first time in the work, he broods over his mother's death in
childbirth, and his own lack of a father. He hears the song of a
bird in the forest and tries to answer it, but after vain attempts
blows on his horn instead, calling the dragon from the cave. He
stabs him with his sword and Fafner, reverting to his own shape,
tells Siegfried his history.

As Siegfried withdraws his sword, blood from the dragon falls
on his lips; tasting it he finds he can understand the song of the
wood-bird, which tells him to take from Fafner's cave the ring
and Tarnhelm. Mime and Alberich quarrel over the treasure but
break off as Siegfried returns. The bird speaks again to Siegfried,
putting him on his guard against Mime's hypocritical deceit.

Mime seeks to lull Siegfried's suspicion: but the blood allows Siegfried (and the audience) to hear him spelling out his true murderous intentions. In disgust Siegfried kills him. Wearily he lies down under the tree, and again hears the bird's advice: he is to set out to the mountain-top, pass through the ring of fire and claim his promised bride. He follows the bird as it leads the way.

The third act starts at the foot of the mountain. Wotan summons Erda, seeking to know the secrets of the future. She suggests he ask their daughter: he realises that she had not even known of Brünnhilde's fate. Perceiving that divine wisdom has had its day, Wotan claims that he is happy to meet his own end and bequeath his inheritance to Siegfried, confident that Siegfried is the truly independent hero of his wishes. Siegfried, appearing, is engaged in conversation by the wanderer: becoming increasingly impatient with the old man, he shatters the spear he places in his path.

Siegfried proceeds into the wall of fire and, as the second scene begins, emerges from it on the top of the mountain. He sees the form of the sleeping Brünnhilde. At first taking her for a male warrior, he realises as he removes her breastplate that she is a woman. He begins to know the meaning of fear; and, expressing it and overcoming it at once, kisses her on the lips. She wakes, greets the light and greets Siegfried, telling him that she has always loved him, even before his birth. Siegfried guesses that she is his mother but she explains her role in protecting his real mother. Siegfried embraces her; she fears a human's embrace and begs him not to destroy the purity of her loving care for him. His desire increases, and she is won over. Brünnhilde bids farewell to the Gods.

Siegfried: *Commentary*

The preludes to the first and second act of *Siegfried* may include some of the earliest surviving music from Wagner's first sketches of the entire cycle. The third act was entirely composed after the completion of *Tristan und Isolde* and *Die Meistersinger*. Thus the work might be expected to cover a stylistic span so great as to lead to incoherence. Stylistic disparity is in fact greatest in the second act; on the other hand this act is the most eventful single section in the entire *Ring*, and the close involvement of its music with its action confers a dramatic effectiveness on the style which more than fulfils Wagner's ultimate programme. Wagner considered abandoning the opera at the point where Siegfried, having killed Mime, lay under the tree; but he in fact completed the music for the second act before devoting his energies to *Tristan*. Act Two marks, rather precisely, the point where the destructive energies of the hero, directed against an old world

Lauritz Melchior as
Siegfried, Bayreuth
1928.

inherited from the earlier operas, pass over into potentially
creative and self-creative energies, dedicated to love and the new
human worlds which it may open out. It is not surprising that
Wagner should have felt a need to develop and enhance his
harmonic imagination, and perhaps also his emotional freedom
in composition, before returning to the world of the *Ring*.

It is striking how successfully Wagner, in Act Three, picks up
the themes and the harmonic language of the earlier parts of the
cycle. The great advance marked out by the third act of *Siegfried*
is indicated by the immensely powerful combination of themes
revealed in the orchestral prelude. In the extended love-duet,
making up the last twenty minutes or so of the opera's action,
the harmonic language associated with Tristan and Isolde is

119

carefully excluded from the very different love between Siegfried and Brünnhilde. These last twenty minutes deploy a thematic language not heard previously in the *Ring*, some of it not to be heard again, including themes familiar in orchestral guise in Wagner's *Siegfried Idyll*. The love between Siegfried and Brünnhilde, in one sense the dramatic climax of this work and of the human vision of the cycle up to this point, is thus in another sense curiously marginal to the onward movement of the cycle. It also involves the tenor hero in the most strenuous vocal demands of the whole work, which, coming after three-and-a-half-hours during which he is rarely absent from the stage, have made the part more nearly unperformable than that of any other Wagnerian protagonist.

The drama of the first two acts involves frequent narrations of past events. These, to a greater extent than in *Die Walküre*, are presented in the guises of conversation, argument or game. These two acts recall in many ways the comparatively clear-cut thematic language of *Das Rheingold*, and present characters absent from *Die Walküre* but present in the earlier work – Alberich, Mime, Fafner and (in the third act) Erda. It is dramatically and musically appropriate that the product of all the recapitulatory material of the first act should be the forging of a new tool; similarly, that in the second act the hero, setting behind him the contests of Wotan and Alberich, moves through a passive acceptance of natural beauty into a powerfully active response – his victory over Fafner and his ability to communicate with the wood bird. The climax of Siegfried's heroic education, in the second act, lies in his seizing of the initiative, first against Mime, and more positively in pursuit of the promised bride. At the climax of the act, the hero is thus fully invested in the powers of nature and of individual culture, and looks forward to the different fulfilments offered by human society.

The great explicit dramatic theme of *Siegfried* is that of fear, its value and its limitations. The ideal hero will be free from fear; but such a hero would be less than human. Mime fears, Fafner has reason to fear; even the defiance enunciated by Alberich, and implied by Wotan's apparent self-confidence, is rooted in a past history of claim and counterclaim which has left them both with good reason to fear the other – and to fear supersession by their sons. Siegfried, shattering Wotan's spear, fulfils at once Wotan's fear and his deepest desire; passing beyond fear, he equally passes beyond history. But Brünnhilde, who teaches him fear, carries a history with her, involving her own rejection of divine morality and her embrace of an unknown future. The uncertain balance between openness and self-protectiveness, embodied in the ending of *Die Walküre*, is

Siegfried Act Two, at Bayreuth in 1952; Renaissance man meets a modern dragon.

thus again dramatised in the relationship between Siegfried and Brünnhilde at the end of this drama. The lovers in their last words expose themselves to 'laughing death'; is this an acceptance of mortality, chance and human history, or is it (as Wagner's reading of Schopenhauer may have led him to feel) a rejection of these things? If the latter, it is striking that the entire cycle does not in fact end here. History and fear were not to be so suddenly or freely abandoned as Siegfried, or as Wagner, may have hoped; the legacy of the 1848 plans for the *Ring*, involving as they did precisely a reckoning with the structures of human history, remained, for Siegfried and for Brünnhilde to encounter in the final work of the cycle.

Götterdämmerung: *Plot*

In the first scene of the Prologue, set on the mountain top, the three Norns, daughters of Erda, weave the rope of destiny. They tell of Wotan's search for wisdom, of Siegfried's destruction of Wotan's spear, and of how Wotan sent heroes from Valhalla to chop down the world ash tree. The logs of the tree have been piled around Valhalla: one day they will be ignited in flames. The end of the gods is present to the Norns in their vision, but not the role of Alberich or of the Rhinegold. As they brood on this, the rope of destiny breaks. They descend into the earth. Dawn breaks. Siegfried and Brünnhilde emerge from their cave. Siegfried must proceed to new heroic deeds. He gives Brünnhilde the ring as a token of their love; Brünnhilde offers him her horse. He rides off on his journey down the river Rhine.

The first act begins in the hall of the Gibichungs, where Gunther, their chief, asks his half-brother, Hagen, how he may guarantee and maintain his reputation. Hagen, who is Alberich's son (by a human woman), and Gunther's half-brother, tells Gunther that he should marry, as should his sister Gutrune. To Gunther he holds out hopes of Brünnhilde, but tells him she lives surrounded by fire on a mountain top. For Gutrune he extends the possibility of Siegfried's love, while concealing Siegfried's commitment to Brünnhilde. Siegfried arrives and is welcomed. Hagen recognises him as the possessor of the Nibelung's treasure; Siegfried says that he left it in the cave, taking only the Tarnhelm. Gutrune gives him a drink in which, at Hagen's suggestion, she has inserted a love-drug; Siegfried, drinking to the memory of Brünnhilde, (whose name is not heard by Gutrune or Gunther), immediately falls in love with Gutrune and offers himself as her husband. He also offers to be Gunther's champion and to win Brünnhilde, disguising himself, with the help of the helmet, as Gunther. Gunther and Siegfried swear brotherhood and loyalty to one another. Hagen, as they leave, broods over his schemes for control of the palace and of the gold.

In the second scene Brünnhilde, contemplating her love for Siegfried, is interrupted by one of her fellow Valkyries, Waltraute, who tells her that Wotan, resigned to the end of the gods' power, longs for the ring to be returned to the Rhinemaidens. Brünnhilde refuses to throw away the token of her love. After Waltraute's departure, her calm is broken by Siegfried's horn, and his arrival in the guise of Gunther. He claims Brünnhilde as 'his' wife, snatches the ring from her finger and draws her for the night into the cave. Alone, he pledges fidelity to Gunther's interests: his drawn sword will separate him from Brünnhilde.

The second act is set again outside the hall of the Gibichungs. Hagen, half-asleep, is visited by his father Alberich. He promises to gain the ring, but makes no commitment to restore it to Alberich. Siegfried, at dawn, returns, now in his own shape, and tells Hagen and Gutrune of his success. Hagen calls Gunther's vassals to celebrate two impending weddings. Gunther arrives leading Brünnhilde as his reluctant bride. When he names the second wedding couple as Gutrune and Siegfried, Brünnhilde, horrified, asks whether Siegfried has forgotten her. He denies ever having known her; when she asks him how he acquired the ring, he claims simply to have won it from the dragon. She explodes in anger at his betrayal and at the gods who have allowed it. She claims Siegfried as her husband. Siegfried reveals his role in winning Brünnhilde for Gunther and claims to have had no physical relations with her. She denies this passionately. They swear counter-oaths, on the point of Hagen's spear. Siegfried tries to pass the affair off lightly, as a typical instance of women's volatile emotions. As the vassals follow him into the hall, Brünnhilde laments his treachery and eventually accepts Hagen's offer of revenge. She tells him that Siegfried can be wounded and killed with a blow to his back. Gunther is won over to the plan by a promise of the ring.

The third act begins on the banks of the river Rhine, where the Rhinemaidens reappear, still lamenting the loss of their gold. They greet Siegfried and ask him for the ring, which he now wears on his finger. He refuses their advances but then offers it to them in playful love. They warn him of the danger to which any holder of the ring is exposed. Siegfried fears no external threats and retains the ring.

A hunting party, led by Hagen, arrives. Siegfried drinks with them. Gunther guiltily broods over impending events. Siegfried tells Hagen and Gunther the full story of his life, from his education by Mime, through his heroic deeds; as Hagen gives him a drink, which reminds him of all he has forgotten, he proceeds to tell of his love for Brünnhilde. Gunther is horrified. Hagen plunges his spear into Siegfried's back. Siegfried dies, singing Brünnhilde's name, and is carried in procession by the hunting party back to the hall of the Gibichungs.

In the last scene, Gutrune, alarmed by Siegfried's absence, encounters the returning Hagen followed by Siegfried's funeral procession. Gunther, accused by his sister of Siegfried's death, blames Hagen; Hagen claims that Siegfried had deserved death for betraying both Brünnhilde and Gunther. He claims the ring; challenged by Gunther, he kills him. He is checked by the hand of the dead Siegfried, rising from his body. Brünnhilde, entering, orders the vassals to set up a funeral pyre for the dead hero. She understands his betrayal; but Siegfried has atoned for his guilt in death, and has given her a full understanding of the nature of humanity, learnt through grief. She promises that the ring will be returned to the Rhinemaidens, and ignites the pyre. On her horse she rides into the flames. The palace catches fire. The waters of the river rise and flood the area. The Rhinemaidens seize the ring from Siegfried's body. Hagen leaps into the water in pursuit. They drag him down and hold the ring in triumph over him. The firelight rises. In the clouds fire can be seen engulfing the castle of the gods. Valhalla burns in flames. The end of the gods has come and the waters wash over the cleansed human world.

Götterdämmerung: *Commentary*

Despite a number of subsequent revisions, the drama's structure reflects much of Wagner's earliest thinking on the whole scenario of the cycle. As many commentators have pointed out, it also contains more elements of traditional operatic musical and dramatic style than the works which eventually preceded it: powerful choruses in the second act, which ends with an effective trio, and a number of extended opportunities for soloists: Hagen's meditation at the end of Act One Scene I, Siegfried's narration and death in the third act, and, above all, Brünnhilde's final immense aria. It also contains two fine separable orchestral numbers: Siegfried's 'Journey down the Rhine', which carries the music from the Prologue into the first act, and, between the two scenes of the third act, Siegfried's funeral march.

Despite, and because of, these structural elements the work is tightly knit and to some extent concentrically organized, centring on the scenes of confusion, betrayal and self-betrayal at the heart of Act Two. Though this is the shortest act in the entire cycle, it is also the one whose dramatic and musical sweep is most powerfully climactic, as the characters gather on stage in increasing numbers. Such 'operatic' dramaturgy is as effective as anything in Wagner – one token, among many, of the extent to which Wagner's later theories concerning music-drama absorbed, rather than rejecting, his earlier operatic achievement. The work is equally full of those narrations which pervade *Siegfried* and *Die Walküre* – new narrative elements presented by the Norns, the subtly misleading narratives of Hagen in the first scene, and the powerful narrative of Waltraute, which yet fails to persuade Brünnhilde, in the second scene. Siegfried's narration in the third act marks the climax of his heroic career and shows the connection within Wagner's dramatic thought between spontaneous heroism and meditative reflection.

There are few new musical themes in the work; but the final theme has been heard only once before in the cycle, associated with Sieglinde's rapture at the thought of the hero to whom she will give birth. It could be associated with that vulnerable exposure of oneself to an unknown future of which both Sieglinde and the surviving anonymous humans, at the end of the cycle, offer powerful stage images.

Chapter 8

The Ring

The Bayreuth première of the complete *Ring* in August 1876
marks the climax of Wagner's life. It was one of the two or three
major events in the history of musical performance in the
nineteenth century and perhaps the most star-studded social
event in the whole century's artistic calendar. Twenty-eight years
of Wagner's life stretched behind it, through which he had
meditated, theorized, written and re-written, composed and re-
composed, interpreted and constantly re-interpreted his vast but
– as he was determined that the Bayreuth performances should
reveal – single and coherent musico-dramatic conception. The
work was required to make good half a lifetime of isolation,
anxiety and arrogance; of love, dependence and treachery
towards friends, patrons and wives; of calculations disguised as
creative spontaneity and of creativity laboriously vindicating
itself by theoretical calculations. The ambitious discoveries of
Wagner the philosopher had in the end to make themselves
answerable to the diplomatic skills and risk-takings of Wagner
the courtier, and, at the laborious final stage, the immense but
finite practical energies of Wagner the conductor, repetiteur and
theatre director. He was sixty-three years old. Had it all been
worth it? Did it make sense? What sort of sense did it make?

There have been subsequent attempts at exegesis and interpretation of the *Ring*: but not really all that many, given the work's
scale, complexity and fame. Audiences watching or hearing the
work in a language not their own supply a steady market for
accounts, whose aim is fulfilled by the narration of plot and the
listing of musical themes. Histories of its staging, acting and
(increasingly) recording will multiply. But they encounter the
problems of relevance, posed by all critical descriptions of performances; problems acute in spoken theatre, far more so when
music *and* words are involved. Interviews with directors often
call forth large interpretative claims, but few of these are new.
Many directors declare their use of Marxist categories: fewer
within an interview cover enough of the cycle to test the

categories or the claims. The encouragement lent by the *Ring* to the brief bright ideas of its directors and interpreters is probably a salient fact about it. But it is hard to tell how salient, unless such ideas are pursued coherently.

Is the *Ring* one work or more than one? Wagner designated it a 'Stage Festival Play for three days and a preliminary evening'. The word 'stage' qualifies the word 'play': silent reading, listening to a recording, or watching a video, will not ultimately meet Wagner's demands on his public. The words 'three days and a preliminary evening' in turn may be explicated by the word 'Festival': that is to say, special conditions of public attention are required. Any work of art may be felt to occupy a liminal situation in relation to its public. It approaches them where they are, it draws them to where it is; the two movements may meet or evade each other, but it will be impossible in advance to specify the meeting-place in terms other than those provided by the relationship itself. The work and the public thus become each other's thresholds, boundaries and points of transmutation. A festival may be an attempt at providing a meeting-place without advance reference to particular audiences or works. The *Ring*, for Wagner, was at once a festival and the work for the festival. Even its periodic interruptions for food and drink, meditation and sleep would become part of its festival procedures. It is not so much that the separate days and the evening are linked, however subtly or powerfully, by their dramatic themes; rather the gaps between them draw their audience into contemplation of what, as they separate on their individual businesses, continues to link them, and of what, when they rejoin one another in the festival theatre, will still necessarily divide them.

They will be divided by gender, age, class and nationality. Love and war between genders (one can hardly say 'men and women') begin the 'preliminary evening' *Das Rheingold*, and recur in the cycle's final act. In the final acts of the two intermediate works youth challenges experience: Wotan punishes Brünnhilde, Siegfried shatters Wotan's sphere and ends the conditions of Brünnhilde's punishment. On the other hand Brünnhilde, Wotan's daughter, is, as parodists have made famous, Siegfried's aunt: age and youth meet in her; as do, in *Götterdämmerung*, hostility to Siegfried's typically male sexual treachery, and love which accepts his obligations to 'new deeds' and his contradictory complexity.

Class and the *Ring*

What is the place of class in the *Ring*? Wagner invented the first scene of *Das Rheingold* in which, as Bernard Shaw saw it, the grimy worker Alberich is despised by, and takes predictably

stony-hearted revenge upon, the lazy upper-class Rhinemaidens. The scene has no basis in Teutonic myth: nor does the presentation of the Nibelungs as Alberich's slaves; nor of Mime as his brother, even more cruelly forced to service. When Wotan and Loge drag Alberich from the caves of Nibelheim to the mountain heights in scene four, they allow Alberich's claims against the gods to be heard in the gods' own territory.

Thus in the 'preliminary evening' Wagner goes out of the way of his sources to create one of the most memorable and incisive characters of his entire dramatic output: Alberich, lustful, self-denying and furiously energetic, self-centred to the point of displaying obtuseness about his own vulnerability, but mockingly perceptive of the weaknesses of those placed above him. Such a dramatic achievement embraces, while transcending, allegory. Alberich, who functions in the *Ring* far more variously than a view of him simply as 'worker', 'industrialist' or 'racial inferior' would imply, nonetheless casts brilliant light on the complexity of the dynamic relations between such figures and respectively their 'employers' and 'racial superiors'. *Das*

Rheingold deploys varieties and relationships of place mor
freely, flexibly and clearly than any of the other operas in th
cycle. Within its flexibility 'class' knows, finds and seeks t
change its place.

But *Das Rheingold* also stands somewhat outside the cycle. It
point is the apparent clarification of differences, of class, gende
and species, between which there is to be displayed not only, a
in *Das Rheingold*, hierarchy and mobility, but also, in the cycl
proper, systematic confusion and creative treachery. It is hard t
locate class relationships in the three later works. Alberich's so
Hagen is no industrialist and no second-generation decaden
offspring of industrialists. In his single-minded malevolence he i
a powerful antithesis to Siegfried. But socially he is a frustrate
and marginalised aristocrat, with career horizons limited to th
rewards of powerless wisdom; limited again in an aristocrati
court by his ambiguous paternity. (Thus he is one of Wagner'
most obvious dramatic alter egos). Siegmund is a nomadi
warrior, Siegfried is a child of nature. Gunther and Gutrune ar
feudal aristocrats. They all inhabit a time-frame preceding tha
of Wagner, or of Marx. Class distinctions affect them little – a
against distinctions of status.

Such arguments may be accused of missing the nature o
Wagner's dramatic technique. Alberich, it will be urged, is no
himself an industrialist or an accumulator of primitive capital
but is an allegory, a personalised sign of the operations o
capitalist industry. If so (the reply would run), this sig
functions by virtue of its difference from what it signifies, or (
rather different point) the sign illuminates because it i
irreducible to any one of the several things it signifies. How, fo
example, is Gunther capable of illuminating an audience'
conception of the feudal aristocracy? He is not a sign of it, bu
rather an example of it. It is in fact quite possible, legitimate an
even interesting to analyse the characters of the three main part
of the *Ring* in terms of not so much their class relations as thei
social stratification. The dramas make this explicit. They do no
similarly explicate what such stratification signifies.

This stratification might signify notions of national and racia
division. The claims recently made for seeing Alberich and Mim
as in some sense corresponding to Wagner's conceptions of th
'typical Jew' gain strength, rather than otherwise, from th
distance between character and alleged signification. As alread
said, Wagner alone is responsible for the presentation o
Alberich and Mime as brothers; and the scenarios and texts o
their operas date from years in the early 1850s when he wa
concerned to recommend the self-annihilation of Jewish religiou
and social specificity. A 'Jewish' Mime implies a 'German' Arya
'Siegfried', and perhaps a 'European' but not German pair o

Gibichung siblings. But such interpretations, however close to some of Wagner's beliefs and attitudes, are not likely to be persuasive as general readings of the cycle. National and racial divisions, while they are not overtly displayed in the text of the *Ring*, as are divisions of status, do not seem either to be consistently connoted by the operation of its signifying systems.

I have already suggested that the three main music-dramas are concerned, unlike *Das Rheingold*, with confusions of age and gender role. They also present characters of very different status and biological origin encountering one another in ways subtle or violent, whose effect is not, as in *Das Rheingold*, to confirm, but to overturn division and hierarchy. Incestuous love between Siegmund and Sieglinde challenges the conventional laws of marriage and sexual availability. Brünnhilde's support of Siegmund against Hunding defies her father and seeks to divert the claims of legitimate property, for Siegmund has stole Sieglinde, Hunding's wife and therefore Hunding's possession. In this Brünnhilde is also diverting the demands of divine will. She thus subverts the force of her own divine parentage. Her arguments in turn modify the choice, and the finality, of Wotan's punishment of her. Siegfried forges the unforgeable sword, kills the unconquerable dragon, understands the incomprehensible language, and passes the impassable fire, while Wotan conceals his inalienable identity, Erda's inexhaustible resources of wisdom are exhausted and Fafner the dragon proves human at the last.

A pattern of overturning

If the dwarf Mime is, despite all this, true to his nature, that nature itself is given to both deception and subversion. His greed for power is no more obviously reprehensible than that of his brother Alberich: his hatred of his brother is closer to ambition than to the servility of his role in *Rheingold*; and his close adherence to Siegfried invites an interpretation stressing parallels as well as differences between Siegfried and himself. They are both tenors, both smiths, both forest dwellers, both under Wotan's surveillance and both affected by the death of Fafner and the advice of the wood bird. Mime, until his last moments, fears Siegfried and much else; while Siegfried, hoping to learn fear from Mime, learns it from Brünnhilde, Mime's ultimate successor as his tutor. Such parallelisms are as great an overturning of an audience's assumptions about hierarchy and division as anything else in the whole cycle.

The pattern of overturning continues in *Götterdämmerung*; plans and conspiracies are affected by the love of a woman: Siegfried's free heroic will and freely submissive love for Brünnhilde are deflected by his sexual desire for Gutrune. An old aristocratic class, represented by the Gibichungs, together with their vassals, their palace and their oaths, is destroyed by the new social energies represented by Siegfried, the child of nature, by Brünnhilde herself, the woman who has never known bondage to any human society, and finally by the untrammelled natural forces of fire and water. Even the power and will of the gods are subverted by the commitment of Brünnhilde to a human love.

But an analysis of *Götterdämmerung* in terms of overturning and of the release of revolutionary subversive energies must confront the sense of oppression, contradiction and tragedy which much of the opera purveys. Above all, the Siegfried of *Götterdämmerung* appears regularly in performance as a radically diminished figure by comparison with the figure of the earlier drama; diminished by contact with aristocratic civilisation and with human collectivity in general, and particularly diminished by the charges of treachery to which he seems deservedly vulnerable after the operations of Hagen's love potion. Brünnhilde herself has also often been seen as diminished, by stooping to collaboration with such limited and vitiated characters as Gunther and Hagen. The aesthetic design of *Götterdämmerung* has frequently been seen as, in damaging ways, a throwback to the dramaturgy of Wagner's operas of the 1840s; a return from the revolutionary ideals of music-drama to the more old-fashioned and conventional ethos of grand opera.

But the extent to which this style limits Wagner's achievement, either in *Götterdämmerung* itself or in the *Ring* cycle as a whole, deserves further consideration. A positive view of Wagner's dramaturgy in the works of the 1840s might encourage a more positive evaluation of these features of *Götterdämmerung* and of the contribution that it makes to the *Ring* cycle.

The operas of the 1840s, which clearly retain many traditional musical set-pieces, employ them to present human confrontations, contradictions between humans and the societies to which they are bound, and self-contradictions. This aesthetic, which remains central to *Götterdämmerung*, allows one to see its early date as making for a positive rather than a negative view of its place in the *Ring*.

Das Rheingold depicts a number of different species – Rhinemaidens, dwarfs, giants, gods and goddesses – in order to communicate, by allegory, a view of the separation and alienation of vital human energies from one another. Nature and natural beauty (the Rhinemaidens) are alienated from ambitions towards morality and aesthetics (the gods). Such ambition in turn is liable to run counter to the desire for contented sexual love (Fricka) and the illusion of self-renewing youth. Estranged from all these stands the malignly creative figure of Alberich, embodying the human potential for recreating society on the basis of material possession and social oppression. Over against all the other characters stands the enigmatic and central figure of Loge: a god, and yet only ambiguously a god; an intellectual, indeed – as has often been observed – the only intellectual in the whole of the *Ring* cycle, and yet one whose instincts lead him to take the side of the profoundly unintellectual Rhinemaidens, and to urge upon Wotan their plea for the return of the gold and the ring. His help to the gods, indispensable as it is, seems to be given entirely on a temporary basis, committing him to no long-term alliance with them or with anyone else. In Loge we have a figure for the nature of *Rheingold* as a drama in general; a figure, that is, for the separation of human powers one from another. Such separation is communicated by allegory and in a mode of sharply ironic comedy.

Now in *Götterdämmerung*, which by its representation of the Rhinemaidens immediately evokes memories of the beginning and end of *Das Rheingold*, we encounter a dramatisation of this same separation of human powers in the form of tragedy. It is no coincidence that the music associated with Loge and with the notion of fire (at once intellectually creative and socially destructive) recurs at the end of *Götterdämmerung*, just as the visual image of fire is, according to Wagner's instructions, one of the dominant stage images at the end of the opera.

Human and heroic love

But, between the first and the last works of the cycle, Wagner's dramaturgy has proceeded, not in terms of allegory, with the implied separateness between human powers, and between signifier and signified, that allegory involves; rather it has proceeded in two exemplary and essentially human dramatic actions: in *Die Walküre* and in *Siegfried*. *Die Walküre* depicts the course of a human and heroic love between Siegmund and Sieglinde which, running as it does into conflict with divine law, nonetheless has the power to force self-division upon the chief of the gods and to lead his daughter to an alliance with the lovers and, in their persons, with humanity. This ultimately leads her to a change of species-being, from a divinity to a human woman.

The tragic fate of human love, already apparent in *Die Walküre*, is further exemplified by the course of Brünnhilde and Siegfried's love in *Götterdämmerung*. Between these two works the opera *Siegfried* has offered a different set of human values as the subject of a further exemplary human action; the values, that is, of Siegfried's fearless and equally (until the end of the work) loveless human revolutionary energy. Siegfried, for many, is an uncomfortable heroic character. I would argue that this is an appropriate response to what Wagner himself has offered in the work, rather than a response precluding any enjoyment of the work. Siegfried, who (as already suggested) undergoes a potentially limiting parallelism and comparison with Mime, is also, until the end of the work, impervious to those values which have come to be embodied by Brünnhilde. In that he is the child of loving parents, Siegmund and Sieglinde, Siegfried is also more generally limited by a refusal to understand his own past which leads him to re-enact and re-experience it. Thus the apparent joyful freedom of Siegfried's heroic self-discovery and self-expression is qualified, both in advance and in prospect, by the tragic, though appreciative, presentation of human love.

In *Götterdämmerung* the limits of exemplary human action are revealed, as the forces of heroic energy and human love collide with one another, in the persons of Siegfried and Brünnhilde and in the tortured course of their relationship. The causes of this collision are shown to lie in their involvement with human society at large. The limitations of the court of the Gibichungs, in its aristocracy, its sense of social immobility, and its moral medievalism, may be seen as endemic to a typically German audience. Indeed, in many ways Wagner may have seen the Gibichungs as the embodiment of those most frustrating aspects of the audience to which the whole cycle itself is directed. In this view the disjunctive nature of the dramaturgy of *Götterdämmerung* is an appropriate image for the separations of gender, class, age and in some senses nationality, which were, and still are, inevitably present in any audience of the opera and of the cycle. It is a measure of the greatness of the cycle that it refuses to force upon its audience any illusory transcendence of these contradictions; and, similarly, it is the greatness of Wagner's musical dramaturgy that in this last work it allows an audience to perceive, through the tight interconnections of theme and character, the styles (including the use of separate numbers) of the whole of his earlier career.

I have offered an interpretation of the *Ring* cycle which seems exposed to one very obvious objection; this is a *Ring* without the ring. The symbol of the ring, I would suggest, embodies, at a powerfully simple level, both the continuities and the discontinuities of the work and of its audiences as a whole. A ring is an image of power and of control. The allegory of *Das Rheingold* requires an audience to accept a necessary separation between powerful control and spontaneous love. On the other hand the ring is fashioned out of the gold which, under the guardianship of the Rhinemaidens, is already present within nature. The separation between power and love propels the ironic comedy of *Das Rheingold*. This in turn propels attempts to overcome the separation, embodied in *Die Walküre*, whose presiding deity is love, and *Siegfried,* whose presiding deity is energy.

Richard and Cosima Wagner photographed in 1872 by Fritz Luckhardt.

The clash between these two central operas and their systems of value is then brought to a head in *Götterdämmerung*. Its final act confronts Siegfried with the choice faced in *Das Rheingold* by Wotan and Alberich. The Rhinemaidens beg Siegfried to return the ring to them. He refuses to do so because of his commitment to love. An irony here lies in the fact that his beloved is Gutrune, as he supposes, rather than Brünnhilde. Yet the irony expresses a deeper necessity. There is no return to nature and illusory unity available to the characters of this profoundly human and socially contradictory drama; and when at the end of the work the ring is almost perfunctorily restored to the Rhinemaidens by Brünnhilde, the result is not (though some have found this strange) the overcoming of human conflict, or of divine necessity, in a spurious unity, but rather the emergence of those natural energies of fire and of water which were dormant at the start of the whole cycle but whose energies have given rise to, and have been deployed by, human society at large. Fire and water join with the gold of the ring to destroy, and to leave the room clear for a new possible creation. Its guiding principles may well be those of love, but they must also embody the intellectual and critical awareness identified with the figure of Loge.

In the 1852 version of the text of the end of *Götterdämmerung* lines were present which Wagner later deleted; their motto lies in the following phrase:

'blessed in joy and sorrow only love may be'.

In 1856 Wagner changed his intended text to one whose lines include the following phrases:

'*I depart from the home of desire, I flee forever from the home of delusion, the open gates of eternal becoming I close behind me. Grieving love's deepest suffering opened my eyes. I saw the world end*'

This too was deleted. The 1852 lines have become known as the 'Feuerbach' ending, the 1856 as the 'Schopenhauer' ending. The *Ring* includes and transcends them both. It encourages sympathy and admiration for its lovers, but holds out to them no expectation either of worldly reward or of other-worldly escape. Power, in its self-imposed blindness and its resentment of others, will always, despite the best of intentions, limit love and freedom. But there can be no return to nature which is not also a return to culture, to power and to human social difference. It is the refusal of the cycle to support circular, self-justifying inter-pretations which gives it the ring of truth.

Chapter 9

Sage and Invalid

Top row, left to right: Blandine von Bülow (daughter of Cosima and Hans), Heinrich von Stein (writer for *Bayreuther Blätter*), Cosima Wagner, Richard Wagner. Bottom row, left to right: Isolde Wagner (daughter of Cosima and ?Richard), Daniela von Bülow (daughter of Cosima and Hans), Eva Wagner and Siegfried Wagner (children of Cosima and Richard). On the right, between the rows: Paul von Joukowsky, stage designer for *Parsifal*.

At the 1876 performances of the *Ring*, Wagner arranged matters so that he was able to sit in the darkened theatre next to Judith Gautier. His close involvement with her continued for the next two years, under the watchful eye of Cosima. Was this a new emotional world for Wagner or a late return of old patterns? Such questions emerge constantly through any consideration of the last six or seven years of Wagner's life.

His final meeting with Nietzsche took place in October 1876; from now until the end of his own philosophical career, Nietzsche's denunciations of Wagner and Wagnerism were to become strident, and (one must grant) increasingly philosophically powerful and creative. The *Ring* cycle had left a debt of 148,000 marks – the contemporary equivalent of £7,400. In May 1877 Wagner undertook the conducting of yet another series of London concerts, in the newly opened Royal Albert

Hall, but the £700 that they realised went very little way to clearing this deficit. In the same year as the Bayreuth cycle, he was commissioned to compose a centennial march for the hundredth anniversary of the founding of the United States, and fantasy projects of emigration to the United States were much in his mind in 1877. The hectic creative and promotional energies of the earlier 1870s were taking a considerable, if belated, toll.

Even the artists and writers who were delighted to encounter Wagner in London in 1877 formed a telling mixture of older and younger generations, and of past and of future tastes and tendencies. Alongside Robert Browning was George Eliot, alongside Queen Victoria was the pre-Raphaelite Burne-Jones and the future socialist and Marxist, William Morris. Wagner's own political and polemical interests had moved far from the radicalism of the late 1840s. In January 1878 a new journal entitled the *Bayreuther Blätter* was founded, as a vehicle for the writings of Wagner, of his followers and of those studying and promoting his work. Its editor, invited to Bayreuth for this purpose, was Hans von Wolzogen, who continued in this post until his death in 1938. By that time another of Wagner's greatest admirers was securely in control of the German people. The first of Wagner's writings published in the journal, in March 1878, was entitled 'Modern'; the title concealed a strenuous denunciation of the supposed Jewish domination of modern culture and an implicit call for Germans to reclaim and bring to fruition their own traditional and independent cultural property.

The financing of the *Ring* deficit was at last settled in March 1878 by an agreement with King Ludwig, who reasserted his sole right to the production of Wagner's works and to any receipts that might subsequently accrue through any of these productions. Ludwig in fact, with remarkable generosity, set aside for Wagner's own use ten per cent of all receipts until such time as the overall debt should be cleared. The king would have set more store by the right, also secured in this agreement, to have Wagner's new opera *Parsifal* eventually performed, if not at Munich, then by the artists of the Munich court theatre. An unintended consequence of this agreement was the conductorship of Hermann Levi, a Jew and one of Wagner's staunchest admirers, at the eventual Bayreuth première of *Parsifal* in July 1882.

Parsifal, the great achievement of Wagner's last years, was another project with roots firmly set in the past. Wagner had been reading legends and medieval poetry associated with the story of Parzifal as early as his holiday at Teplitz in Bohemia in 1845. The conception of an opera in its own right can be traced as early as 1857, and in August 1865 Wagner constructed a prose draft which in Christmas 1869 he read to Nietzsche.

Hermann Levi, the Jewish conductor of the Bayreuth *Parsifal*.

Nietzsche's responses to *Parsifal* lie near the heart of his increasingly critical stance towards Wagner's work in the 1870s. A second prose draft was completed in February 1877, and by April the text had achieved its poetic form. Wagner set himself to the musical composition in November 1877 and the basic draft of composition was complete by April 1879. The prelude to the work was orchestrated at a relatively early stage, in the autumn of 1878; Wagner conducted it in a private performance for Ludwig at the court theatre in Munich in November 1880. On this occasion Wagner and Ludwig met for the last time. The orchestration of the opera as a whole proceeded from August 1879 to completion in January 1882. It was clear to Wagner at this time, and to the European world of his admirers, that *Parsifal* was to be Wagner's musico-dramatic last will and testament.

Anti-Semitic tracts

Through these years of subtle and fruitful musical composition two other patterns dominate Wagner's late life. On the one hand he poured out a stream of increasingly violent prose polemic whose topics, though ostensibly removed from *Parsifal,* and even further from his earlier music-dramas, may be found damagingly pertinent to the interpretation of these works. The Bayreuth devotees of Wagner, after his death, made little distinction between the authoritative status of the operas and of the pamphlets, early, middle or late; thus the reception of this constant stream of anti-Semitic tracts forms a crucial topic in a consideration of Wagner's achievement.

In 'Public and Popularity' (1878), Wagner urged Christian theologians to relinquish the importance hitherto attached to Jehovah, considered purely as the God of the Old Testament, leaving available the divine humanity of Jesus for religious belief, and enabling acceptance of the new world-picture promoted by nineteenth century science. In 'Religion and Art' (1880), Christ again occupied a crucial place in Wagner's thinking, considered as a representative of the pure blood which in the thought of Wagner and other German and European conservative intellectuals, alone guaranteed the health and survival of Northern European races. For Wagner, Christianity represented a sequence of progressive decay from the pure blooded nature represented by Jesus. The pervasive influence of Judaism in contemporary culture indicated the consummation of that decay. It was thus necessary for Wagner to urge the likelihood that Jesus was not himself Jewish. In 'Know Thyself' (1881), he argued that German national purity had deteriorated while the pure-bred Latins produced the best form of human character; but Jewish character had not itself decayed, despite its power to infiltrate other national characters and blood stock with decay, but instead remained remarkably consistent across the centuries.

In 'Heroism and Christianity' (1881), Wagner adopted, and also argued with, the racial ideas of the French writer Count Gobineau, whom Wagner met and talked with at length at Bayreuth in May of that year. Gobineau, postulating a hierarchy of races, thought that sexual contact between them, which in his view amounted to miscegenation, was a tragic necessity of historical development. Wagner gave to this conception a turn relevant to the dramatic narrative of *Parsifal*. Redemption from the downward spiral of miscegenation could only be brought about through an infusion of the supremely pure blood of Jesus Christ. The apparent rite of communion in the first act of *Parsifal* embodies such a partaking of blood, and thus offers a paradoxical fusion of Christian and racist ideologies.

Wagner's anti-Semitism, though by no means universal in German intellectuals of his time, was shared with many writers whose disappointment in German cultural life after the political triumph of 1871 had turned them from supportive optimism to critical and reactionary pessimism. The Jews were one among various available scapegoats in the construction of new styles of historical philosophy which sought an explanation for the failure of cultural nationalism to live up to the opportunities provided for it by the political triumphs of the German nation.

It has often been noted that Wagner normally showed little or no hostility to individual Jews. A number of Jews, within and outside Wagner's acquaintance, were themselves hostile to the traditional observances of Jewish religion and to the reservation of any distinct status in civil life for Jews. Such assimilationists frequently condemned traits of Judaism in tones which in the mouths of a non-Jew could only be called anti-Semitic. The desire for integration, both visible and subconscious, within the powerful machines of German cultural and civil life is particularly visible in the career of Hermann Levi, the first conductor of *Parsifal* in 1882.

Wagner's anti-Semitism took an unusually theological line in argument. It may have owed this to his constant dealings in his operas with overtly Christianised subject matter. But it also conferred upon subsequent anti-Semitic ideology the potential for collusion with organs of official Christianity, which may have prepared for the lack of resistance, within the churches as elsewhere, to official Nazi anti-Semitism in the 1930s.

The Palazzo Vendramin Calergi, on the Grand Canal in Venice, where Wagner died in February 1883.

Wagner's praise of Latin culture connects with another significant strand of his late life. Problems with his health, which had never been absent, increased in 1880 to the point where Wagner was advised to travel south in winter in search of milder climates. In January 1880 the family took up residence in a villa overlooking the Bay of Naples, where they stayed until the August of that year. Wagner was enchanted by the gardens of Ravello, from which his subsequent stage designer for *Parsifal*, Paul von Joukowsky, took the design for Klingsor's 'Magic Garden'. A visit in August to Siena Cathedral provided the inspiration for the scenes set in the hall of the Grail knights. The winter of 1880/81 was spent back in Germany, where Wagner attended in May 1881 the first complete performances of the *Ring* cycle in Berlin. In November of 1881 the Wagners arrived in Palermo in Sicily, where they stayed until February 1882. Despite the Mediterranean climate, Wagner underwent chest spasms in December; these were signs of the seriousness of Wagner's heart condition, though not diagnosed as such at the time.

Death in Venice

The last winter of Wagner's life was again spent south of the Alps, in Venice, where the family arrived in September 1882. Venice was now part of an Italy which had achieved its own national unification between 1860 and 1870, paralleling the national cultural potential of Germany itself. Wagner's great counterpart as a mid-nineteenth century opera composer, Verdi, had become as closely identified with Italian culture as Wagner with that of Germany.

A preoccupation with Italy runs in a curious background counterpoint throughout Wagner's life, from his earliest creative output in the 1830s until his death. The panegyric in praise of free love, which is constituted by his second opera *Das Liebesverbot*, is set in Sicily; the first engagement with the theme of political regeneration, in *Rienzi*, is set in medieval Rome. On a visit to La Spezia on the Italian Riviera in 1853, Wagner (as he later recounted) experienced in a dream a vision of rolling waters which conveyed the sound of the low E flat chord with which *Das Rheingold* begins. Although the historical possibility of this account has been questioned by modern scholars, the connection established by Wagner, between the Italian holiday that year and the release of his musical powers on his supreme masterpiece, indicates the importance he attached to an image of Italy. Similar images recur in the lives, and the self-images, of major German creative artists from the eighteenth century to the present day.

Wagner's family and followers occupied a floor on the

Richard Wagner in his last years.

Palazzo Vendramin, on the Grand Canal. On Christmas Eve 1882 Wagner conducted, in honour of Cosima's birthday, his symphony in C major, composed fifty years earlier. He was pleased to perceive how well the construction and themes of the symphony stood up in the context of the late maturity of his own style. The judgement of the old Wagner on the power and symphonic energies of the young Wagner may stand, with respect not only to that symphony, effective and noteworthy as it is, but also to all those pre-1848 operas of Wagner, from which his creative path had, apparently, taken him so far.

On the February 11th 1883 Wagner began an essay to be entitled 'On the Feminine in the Human'. Two days later he had a furious row with Cosima, his wife. This may well have been occasioned by Wagner's plan to arrange the visit of an English singer named Carrie Pringle, who had taken the part of a flower-maiden in the Bayreuth *Parsifal* performances of 1882. Wagner's heart attack on the same day may have been occasioned by his excitement at Carrie Pringle's possible arrival, or by the tensions released between Richard and Cosima in their argument, or both. Some time after three in the afternoon he died. Cosima had her arms around him.

His body was taken from Venice to Bayreuth by rail. On February 18th it was buried in the house at Wahnfried. Was this an illusion of peace? Or was it peace found finally in artistic illusion?

Parsifal: *Plot*

The first act begins in a forest clearing. Two sleeping knights are woken by the old knight Gurnemanz. Their duty is to guard sacred relics – the Grail, which was the cup used by Christ at his last supper, and in which his blood was caught when it fell from his body on the cross; and the spear, with which, on the cross, Christ's side was pierced.

The knights prepare the bath for their sick king, Amfortas, the guardian of the Grail. Healing ointment is brought for him by the mysterious woman Kundry, helper and mocker of the Grail community. The king, borne in on a litter, speaks of the saviour promised as his healer – a fool made wise by suffering.

The knights taunt Kundry about her wildness. Gurnemanz tells them of how Amfortas had come to be wounded. Amfortas' father, Titurel, had assembled a brotherhood to guard the relics; he excluded Klingsor – even when he castrated himself, in search of utter purity. In revenge Klingsor created a magic garden, where his flowermaidens sought to seduce the Grail knights. Amfortas, sent to defeat Klingsor, was seduced, wounded and despoiled of the sacred spear. Again the prophecy of the 'pure fool' is recalled.

A young man is dragged in by the knights. He has shot a swan. Rebuked by Gurnemanz, he breaks his bow in anguish. He is ignorant of his own name and origins, knowing only his mother's name 'Herzeleide' ('Heart of Sorrow'). He had wandered from his home in search of adventure. Kundry tells him that his mother is dead; he attacks her and is restrained. As Amfortas is led back to the Grail castle, Gurnemanz leads the young knight thither.

The action moves into the hall of the castle. Knights assemble and Amfortas is carried in. The Grail, covered, is placed on a table. Titurel orders Amfortas to reveal the Grail. Amfortas proclaims his own deep unworthiness and seeks atonement. At Titurel's command the cover is removed and Amfortas consecrates bread and wine, which are distributed to the knights. They sing of their joy in partaking of the bread and wine, while Amfortas is borne out again. Parsifal had clutched his heart in shared sympathy at Amfortas' cry of pain, but cannot speak to Gurnemanz of what he has seen. Gurnemanz brusquely orders him to leave. Again an unseen voice repeats the prophecy of the pure fool.

The second act is set in and around Klingsor's castle. Parsifal is approaching. Klingsor calls Kundry, who is also in his service. She attempts to resist Klingsor's command to seduce Parsifal. Parsifal defeats Klingsor's knights, and enters the magic garden. Flowermaidens seek to seduce him. Kundry stops him, as he breaks away from them, calling his name: 'Parsifal'. She is now transformed into a woman of extreme beauty. She tells Parsifal of having seen him when he was a baby on his mother's breast. His mother had died of grief at his desertion; she offers to console him and replace his mother as object of his love. She kisses his mouth. Parsifal clutches his heart, reminded of Amfortas' cry of anguish. He imagines that Christ is calling on him to save him and to cleanse the community of the Grail knights. He pushes Kundry away. She calls upon him to save her as well; she has wandered the earth since the time of Christ, whom she mocked and blasphemed. Parsifal, knowing that he can save them both only by maintaining his purity, resists her appeals. She calls on Klingsor, who hurls the Spear at Parsifal. Parsifal seizes it and with it makes the sign of the cross. The castle and the garden collapse and vanish.

The third act returns to the kingdom of the Grail, where Gurnemanz, in extreme old age, lives as a hermit. Kundry has returned and lies on the ground stiff and almost dead. She asks only to be allowed to serve. It is Good Friday. A man in armour arrives and, as he takes off his armour, is belatedly recognised by

Joukowsky's setting for the Grail Hall in *Parsifal*.

Gurnemanz as Parsifal. Gurnemanz tells him how Amfortas has refused to unveil the Grail; Titurel is dead and the brotherhood is disheartened. Parsifal is remorseful at his own long absence. Kundry washes his feet. Gurnemanz sprinkles water on his head, and Kundry dries his feet with her hair.

Parsifal notes the seeming contradiction between the beauty of the spring weather and the sorrowful occasion of Good Friday. Gurnemanz answers that it is a day of rejoicing. Christ's self-sacrifice redeems humanity and cleanses nature: nature sees, not God, but man made like God: and nature and man are reconciled.

Again Gurnemanz leads Parsifal, now with Kundry, to the Hall of the Grail. The dead Titurel is carried in, followed by Amfortas, again on a bed. Amfortas refuses to reveal the Grail. The knights threaten him violently and he encourages them to kill him. But Parsifal touches Amfortas's wound with the point of the Spear; he is healed, and hands over to Parsifal his function as Lord of the Grail. Parsifal lifts the Grail; it shines, and light falls upon it from above. Kundry, redeemed, dies at last. Parsifal blesses the knights and a dove hovers above his head. The chorus invoke 'redemption for the redeemer'.

Parsifal: *Commentary*

Despite the opera's length, its demands upon performers are significantly less than those of other mature works by Wagner; its orchestral resources, deployed with immense beauty, are smaller, and its disposition of them more straightforward. Wind, strings and brass are regularly heard as groups separate from one another. The emphasis on rich thematic counterpoint is considerably reduced, by comparison with any of Wagner's operas since the time of *Lohengrin*. The text is largely in prose; there is a certain amount of rhyme, but very little alliteration.

There is a relatively small number of recurrent musical themes. Few of these are linked to individual characters or even to the powerfully symbolic objects around which the drama is organised, though those which are are memorable. Much of the score, particularly in Act One, is harmonically powerful and straightforward in its language, especially that associated with the brotherhood of the Grail and its ceremonial function as guardian of the sacred relics. The language of Kundry's encounter with Parsifal in Act Two comes much closer to the sensuous texture of *Tristan und Isolde*, and to its atmosphere of constant key change; and the orchestral prelude to Act Three approaches a complete absence of tonality as nearly as anything in Wagner. But these more extreme perspectives are resisted and marginalised, by the straightforward harmonic beauty of the Good Friday music at the heart of the act, and by the regular changes from one major key to another, with which the work ends.

The work begins and ends in the key of A flat. Other keys, at a distance of a major or minor third from it, acquire some prominence – the key of C major in association with the Grail ceremonies of Act One, the keys of A flat major and G major in association with the maidens of the magic garden and with Kundry in Act Two. This act, unusually for Wagner's operas, begins and ends in the same key of B minor, again at a distance of a third from the home key of the whole work.

These features to some extent suggest Wagner's age, possible exhaustion and cunning husbanding of his creative compositional resources; or perhaps they indicate his intention of creating a masterpiece to sum up all that he felt his art had come to embody. *Parsifal* is one of the more readily transportable of Wagner's works; but the 30-year embargo which he placed upon performances of it outside Bayreuth (this was broken by the Metropolitan Opera of New York in 1903) suggests that for Wagner the place of performance acquired religious sanctity; rather as the work as a whole not so much imitates or stages the ceremonies of the Christian religion, but offers artistic equivalents for them. Over such ceremonies the characters

Peter Hofmann as
Parsifal, Bayreuth
1980.

preside, and through them they articulate new versions of the
Christian themes of sin, suffering, guilt and redemption. Herein
Wagner set forth his most intimate conception of himself; at
once the would-be redeemer and the would-be redeemed.

The work could be understood as embodying a Christian
message: an ideal purity and innocence, set against a material
world of luxury, guilt and self-indulgence. Yet the innocent
Parsifal of Act One can neither redeem nor understand his own
need for redemption. It is only through experience, of both
vicarious suffering and direct sensual temptation, that he
matures sufficiently to offer help, counsel and release to others.
The frequently repeated motto of 'wisdom acquired through

sympathy', could well be understood in relation to Aeschylus's *Agamemnon*, with its motto of knowledge acquired through suffering; or indeed with reference to the pattern in Goethe's *Faust* whereby redemption is made available not to the sinless or to the orthodox but to the one who strives restlessly for experience.

In this sense the opera could be understood as embodying not Christian tradition but a potentially powerful re-interpretation of elements of Christianity. Wagner emphasised the incarnation as the essential Christian message; but his conception of an ideal community appears in *Parsifal* to be both ascetic and exclusive. The Knights of the Grail long for purity; though their longing is expressed in ways which are threatening and unlikeable, their desire is never repudiated. The difference between inclusion in, and exclusion from, the community appears remarkably arbitrary – Klingsor's longing for ascetic purity had been the greatest of all.

Klingsor's exclusion recalls that of Beckmesser in *Die Meistersinger*, and his dedication to revenge evokes the dynamism of Alberich in *Das Rheingold*. In other ways *Parsifal* resumes features from virtually all of Wagner's earlier works. The wanderings of Kundry recall those of *The Flying Dutchman*; the guilty suffering of the seduced Amfortas echoes the oscillations of Tannhäuser. Parsifal himself had been named as Lohengrin's father, and the later opera can be read as offering a more optimistic, though artificial, solution to the problems of communal reform posed by the earlier tragedy. At one stage Wagner had considered giving the name of Isolde to one of the seductive flower maidens. The prevalence of communal ritual, male choruses and processions links *Parsifal* with *Die Meistersinger*. Like Rienzi, Parsifal regenerates a potentially heroic community. As in *Das Liebesverbot*, an anguished and inadequate ruler is marginalised, but not humiliated, by his successor. And with *Die Feen*, Wagner's first opera of all, *Parsifal* shares the sense of the human power to familiarise the powers of the supernatural world.

Chapter 10

Wagner's Afterlife

Wagner and Nietzsche

The most important figure influenced by Wagner during his lifetime was Friedrich Nietzsche. Wagner died in 1883; Nietzsche went mad in early 1889. Well before Wagner's death, Nietzsche had turned from a passionate devotee of Wagner's music into a passionate critic of Wagner as theatrician, intellectual charlatan and crypto-Christian. A consideration of Wagner's

Friedrich Nietzsche, 1844-1900; philosopher, and Wagner's publicist and bitter enemy.

afterlife may appropriately begin with the progress of Nietzsche's responses.

At the age of seventeen Nietzsche was intoxicated by reading and playing the piano score of *Tristan und Isolde*. He met Wagner at Leipzig in 1868 and subsequently visited Tribschen and Wahnfried on a number of occasions. In 1872 he published, as the first fruits of his professorship of classical theology at the University of Basel, his seminal work *The Birth of Tragedy*. In this he offers a radically innovative discussion of ancient Greek tragedy, in terms of the antitheses maintained between principles associated with the gods Apollo (rationality, grace and serenity) and Dionysus (turbulence, conceptual confusion and sensual intoxication). He then interprets Wagner's work as the contemporary equivalent of Greek tragedy, above all by virtue of Wagner's musical 'Incarnation of the spirit of Dionysus'. In Nietzsche's subsequent philosophical development the god Dionysus, and the characteristics associated with him, bear a large number of interpretations but retain a significant centrality, while the characteristics associated with the god Apollo drop into the background. To this extent the effect created upon Nietzsche by Wagner's mature music, above all that of *Tristan und Isolde*, was an abiding one. Significantly he equated the role of the Greek tragic chorus with that of the Wagnerian orchestra.

A number of factors played smaller but significant parts in Nietzsche's early relationship with Wagner. He had interests, if not ambitions, as a composer himself; he was fascinated by the intellectual and social attractions of Cosima Wagner; it has been plausibly suggested that he found in Wagner a substitute for the father who died when he himself was four. (Wagner was in fact born in the same year, 1813, as Nietzsche's father.) Above all, Nietzsche found in Wagner an example to suggest that creative artistic greatness was possible in the immediate present.

He attended an early performance of the *Ring*: but by 1876 his view of Wagner was changing, and he found it increasingly painful to adapt himself both to these changes and to the demands of conversation with the increasingly solipsistic composer. Insofar as the notion that philosophy is a matter of contestation plays a major role in Nietzsche's thought, Wagner's fundamental importance to him may have been as a rival, against whom he could pit himself and over whom, to his own satisfaction, he could achieve victory.

Nietzsche's contestation of Wagner stressed the extent to which the composer was an improviser, an actor, a man of theatre. In his mature thought Nietzsche increasingly rejected theatre, not so much for its falsity as for its complacent acceptance of falsity as central to its mode of practice. This accusation rebounds, not belittlingly but fascinatingly, against Nietzsche himself; his many deliberate inconsistencies, and his versatility of language and style, have much in common with the practice of both an actor and a writer for the theatre.

A perhaps more substantial argument lay in Wagner's seeming acceptance, or appropriation, of Christianity, for the dramatic construction of *Parsifal* and for the social acceptance which he and Cosima sought through the 1870s and the early 1880s. Atheism and anti-Christianity assumed from an early stage in Nietzsche's thought a central and indeed strident place. Again, his disagreement with Wagner seems likely to have lain, not so much in a fundamental intellectual position, as in the role which Wagner felt it proper, and Nietzsche felt it improper, for dissimulation to occupy in relation to that position. Bayreuth and its aura of religiosity irritated Nietzsche intensely. One can sense here the anxiety of the would-be favourite, finding his intimate access to the master devalued by the popularisation of the master's works.

A central point of hostility between Nietzsche and Wagner lay in Wagner's anti-Semitism. Nietzsche was irritated by Wagner's annoyance at Bismarck's measures allowing civil and religious tolerance for Jews in the Second Empire. Though the conflictual nature of Nietzsche's thought emerges here with some clarity, it is impossible not to identify with his anger in this matter.

Ultimately Nietzsche learnt from Wagner a radical distrust for all theologies, philosophies and would-be artistic religions professing the availability of general redemption for human beings. He also learnt the way in which a will to power operates, the solitude it imposes on its practitioners, and the refuges from such solitude seemingly offered by works of art and by artistic experience in Germany. In these ways he perceived, and resisted, features of Wagner's work to which many disciples, whether or not perceiving them, gladly succumbed.

The earliest Wagnerites, in Germany, France and England, resisted the scientific positivism of their times and, to perhaps an even greater extent, the political tide swinging towards increased liberalism. They welcomed and enjoyed, in Wagner's works, the mingling of sensuous (and sensual) enjoyment with a veil of religious and aesthetic idealism. Many of the most passionate followers of Wagner the writer, theorist, politician and philosopher knew little of music. The intellectual history of Wagnerism in the last decade of Wagner's life, and up to the First World War, takes in far more writers than musicians.

Wagner's musical heirs
But some German composers bear very clear marks of Wagner's influence in their orchestral writing, motivic presentation and

harmonic flexibility. One such composer is Engelbert Humperdinck, whose *Hänsel und Gretel* offers perhaps the most easily acceptable form of Wagnerian opera. Others, who wrote no operas, but were profoundly influenced by Wagner in their orchestral writing, include Anton Bruckner and Gustav Mahler. The great Austrian song composer, Hugo Wolf, a passionate admirer of Wagner's music, displayed in his (frequently very brief) songs the ways in which Wagner's advanced harmonic thinking could be adapted to the sensitive interpretation of texts whose formal qualities lay very far from Wagner's own poetry.

Many of Wagner's most passionate devotees, and most committed enemies, were to be found in Vienna, where Wagnerians and Brahmsians arranged themselves into mutually hostile cults, despite Brahms's own insistence on the abiding importance of Wagner, as a titan amongst his contemporaries. The early work of the great modernist composer Arnold Schoenberg bears clear marks of his admiration of Wagner, both as composer and as author; even Schoenberg's subsequent revolutionary theories concerning musical language and structure are deeply indebted to Wagnerian notions of motivic continuity and thematic relevance.

But perhaps the most interesting and independent German musical follower was Richard Strauss. Born in 1864 in Bavaria, Strauss became acquainted at a very early age with Wagner's music, through his father Franz, a leading horn player in the Munich court orchestra. Strauss's first opera, *Guntram*, is a close imitation of the medieval social context, and of the clarity of motivic language, to be found in *Lohengrin*; his second opera, *Feuersnot*, depicts a creative artist, and erotic hero, modelled equally on the young Wagner and the young Strauss himself.

Strauss's later librettos increasingly developed a critique of the themes of 'redemption' so essential to Wagner. In *Salome* and *Elektra* the protagonists' desires for redemption are viewed not in a tragic or positive but in an ironic light. Strauss's collaboration with the great Viennese dramatist and librettist, Hugo von Hofmannsthal, led him to a form of comic opera in which the *motifs* of Wagner worked hand-in-glove with the ironic and accepting world of Mozartian comedy – *Der Rosenkavalier* being the outstanding example. Such works in turn led to operas in which Greek myth, so fundamental to Wagner's own thinking about opera, was treated by Strauss and his librettists in a mode of self-reflective comedy. Strauss's interpretation of Wagner is a 'strong', radical and deliberately wrong-headed one. His operatic successes indicate the level and quality of energy needed to make appropriate, that is to say inappropriate, use of Wagnerian music-drama.

Long before it influenced Strauss, Wagnerianism had put

Hugo Wolf, 1860-1903; Wagnerian and song composer.

down roots in the soil of French culture. The *Tannhäuser* production of 1861, commanded by Napoleon III and enjoyed by Emile Ollivier (subsequently prime minister of France), evoked an admiring review from Baudelaire. Poets and prose writers were in the vanguard of Wagner's admirers in Paris through the 1870s and 1880s. Wagner was interpreted through theories of symbolism (of correspondences between nature and the emotions), and of the self-contained unity of works of art, which move his notions very far from the dramatic sphere in which he himself couched them. The end-product of French Wagnerianism can be found in the movement known as 'decadence', and in Mallarmé's concept of the linguistic sign which bears no meaning beyond itself. The prevalence of Wagnerian culture in France can be illustrated through the very large number of references to Wagner's music in Proust's great novel *A la recherche du temps perdu*.

Meanwhile many French composers made admiring pilgrimages to Bayreuth, and digested their responses into operas and religious works, Wagnerian in harmonic and sometimes motivic styles. They include Ernest Chausson, whose *Le roi Arthus* (King Arthur) stands out as a rare example of a successful (though largely unknown) opera, not by Wagner, constructed on thorough-going Wagnerian premises; also Henri Duparc who, like Wolf, demonstrated the applicability of Wagnerian harmony and word-setting to the medium of solo song. A more surprising French Wagnerian was Emmanuel Chabrier, composer of heroic and comic operas: Wagner's work raised his ambitions but also evoked his skills in parody. Another French Wagnerian, Léo Délibes, suggests (above all in *Sylvia*) the extent to which an exemplary medium for Wagnerian dramatic ideals could be found in the ballet. Ultimately the most sophisticated and discriminating French interpreter of the Wagnerian musico-dramatic aesthetic was to be Claude Debussy. His great opera *Pelléas et Mélisande* employs a continuous orchestral and motivic texture which is inconceivable without a thorough understanding of the work of Wagner: but the constantly understated setting of the text indicates a radically different solution to questions of psychological interpretation raised by comparable mythological, and emotionally ambiguous, themes.

Russian composers, writers and dramatists of the early twentieth century found, in Wagner's prescriptions for a German national culture, material seemingly applicable to their own situation. The impact of Wagner's *Parsifal* can be found in the greatest of Rimsky-Korsakov's operas *The Legend of the Invisible City of Kitezh*, in which also he powerfully draws upon works of Liszt and Humperdinck. Diaghilev was enormously moved by the mythic elements in Wagner's works; the early ballets of Stravinsky, created in collaboration with Diaghilev, can be compared, in their themes of human sacrifice and mythic redemption, with Wagnerian opera. After the 1917 Revolution the radical and Marxist interpretation of the *Ring* found favour with Lunacharsky, an early commissar for culture in the Soviet state; and the great Soviet director, Eisenstein, an admirer of Wagner's practice and theory of stage direction, mounted a production of *Die Walküre*, ironically, on the occasion of the Nazi-Soviet pact of 1939.

Wagner and literature

Wagner found English admirers even before his visit in 1855. George Eliot heard *The Flying Dutchman*, *Tannhäuser* and *Lohengrin* in performances at Weimar in the summer of 1854. The early poetry of Algernon Swinburne frequently employs themes shared with Wagnerian drama; in particular his poem on the Tannhäuser legend, *Laus Veneris*, may well have been inspired by Wagner's own treatment, which it surpasses in both intensity and intellectual interest. Bernard Shaw's music reviews constantly focus on Wagnerian performances in both London and Bayreuth. His five-part drama, *Back to Methuselah*, is avowedly an attempt to follow and surpass Wagner's *Ring*, while the precepts of the revolutionary Wagner are prominent in the so-called 'Revolutionary's Handbook' appended to the published version of Shaw's earlier play *Man and Superman*. In Oscar Wilde's novel *The Picture of Dorian Gray*, the character of Dorian is depicted listening to Wagner's *Tannhäuser*. Aubrey Beardsley, Wilde's younger contemporary, illustrated a number of scenes from Wagner's dramas. The novels of D.H. Lawrence abound in explicit and implicit citations from Wagner's works.

One of the most suggestive dramatic utilisations of Wagner is to be found in a late, problematic play by the great Swedish dramatist August Strindberg. His *Ghost Sonata* is a play in three scenes, thus comparable to traditional symphonic first movements and, perhaps more obviously, to Wagner's mature operas. It is centrally concerned with the possibility of redemption, for selected individuals, from a corrupt and incestuous society of modern materialism and of family in-fighting. Such redemption, as in Wagner's *Parsifal*, is to be found through asceticism and chastity. These prove impossible to maintain. In the first scene, the Old Man, a leading, though malign, character, orders the Student, the sympathetic protagonist of the work, to attend a performance of *Die Walküre*, in order to proceed in his quest for enlightenment. The Old Man, who moves around in a wheelchair, is comparable both to Wotan and to Donner, to whom another character explicitly likens him; he himself speaks of the '*leitmotifs*' which have linked episodes of his life. The final section of Strindberg's play ends not with words, but with music. In such ways Strindberg is offering not an imitation, but an interpretation, of Wagner's work, even a translation of it into a different medium; perhaps the most intelligent and radical transmutation of Wagnerian techniques to be found since the composer's death.

Another major literary figure centrally concerned with Wagner was the great German novelist Thomas Mann. Born in 1875, Mann had early experience of Wagner's music, as indicated in the short story *Tristan*, and more obviously in the famous novella, *Death in Venice* (the place of course of Wagner's own death), in which a leading German writer, holidaying in Venice, falls victim at once to the plague and to a Tristanesque desire for a young boy.

Each of Mann's four major novels can be related to Wagnerian preoccupations and techniques. In *Buddenbrooks* (1901), one of the central characters, Thomas Buddenbrook, depressed in commercial and family relationships, reads Schopenhauer's masterpiece and, like Wagner, experiences the lifting of his burdens. His son, Hanno, misunderstood and neglected by his father, takes refuge in improvisations on the piano, which the novelist describes in terms readily applicable to an experience, like Nietzsche's, of *Tristan und Isolde*. *The Magic Mountain*, for which Mann gained the Nobel Prize in 1929, deploys a tightly interconnected set of intellectual and verbal themes in manners explicitly reminiscent of Wagner's practice of motivic development. *Joseph and his Brothers*, written between 1933 and 1945, is a four-part novel whose construction and vast scale directly evoke comparison with Wagner's *Ring*, while Mann's final full-length masterpiece, *Doctor Faustus*, completed in 1947, presents its ambiguous and dangerous hero in the guise of a German composer of Mann's generation. Comparisons with Arnold Schoenberg and, perhaps more potently, with Robert Schumann have been frequently drawn, but Mann's conception of Faust as a composer shows, also, his continuing involvement with the effects, by this time clearly damaging, of Wagnerism upon German and European culture.

A number of Mann's remarks about Wagner bear quotation:

> Wagner's art is a case of dilettantism that has been monumentalised by a supreme effort of the will and intelligence, a dilettantism raised to the level of genius.

Mann's sense of the theatrical nature of Wagner's art does not lead him to the condemnation found in Nietzsche, whom Mann admired even more intensely and intimately than Wagner, but to a finely nuanced verdict on the relation of Wagner's art to religious ritual:

> . . . An art based on sensuous experience and recurrent symbolic formulae (for the *leitmotiv* is such a formula – more than that, it is a monstrance, laying claim to a authority that verges on the religious) necessarily takes us back to church ceremonial . . . an artist as practised as Wagner in the manipulation of symbols and the elevation of monstrances was bound in the end to see himself as the fellow of the priest – or even as a priest in his own right.

Mann notably avoided seeing in Wagnerism any necessary part of the intellectual and artistic inheritance of his own generation:

> If I try to imagine the artistic masterpiece of the twentieth century, I see something that differs radically – and favourably, it seems to me - from that of Wagner: something conspicuously logical, well formed and clear, something at once austere and cheerful . . . a new classicism, I believe, is on the way . . .

Mann's prophecies, perhaps fulfilled in the work of Brecht

Cosima Wagner in 1918 with Wieland Wagner as a baby.

(who profoundly disliked Thomas Mann and all that he stood for), would have seemed refuted by the survival of Wagnerian production at Bayreuth in traditional and increasingly archaic forms. After Wagner's death, Cosima Wagner, though by no means an obvious artistic heir, succeeded in taking control. Over the next thirteen years she developed productions of *Tristan und*

Isolde, Die Meistersinger and eventually in 1896 the *Ring*, to join the production of *Parsifal* already put in place by Wagner in 1882. In 1907 the son of Richard and Cosima, Siegfried Wagner, took control; a composer of some interest in his own right, he proved a timid, but not entirely unenterprising director and retained power until his relatively early death in 1930. Productions had been interrupted in 1914 and were only resumed in 1924. Siegfried was succeeded by his English-born widow Winifred, a devoted admirer of Hitler. During her regime the Führer regularly attended the festivals. His attendance may have allowed directors at Bayreuth more freedom from Goebbels's control than was enjoyed by most theatres in Germany in the Nazi years. But the damage (in many ways appropriate damage) done to Wagner's reputation by Hitler's self-identification with it was lasting, and remains a powerful factor in the reception of Wagner's work to the present day.

After the Second World War, the Bayreuth stage was dark until 1951, when Wagner's grandsons, Wolfgang and Wieland, inaugurated a new, and in some ways radical, series of productions, which for a couple of decades coincided with the flowering of major vocal talents. Wieland Wagner's productions of *Parsifal, Die Meistersinger* and the *Ring* have become famous for their supposedly non-representational and non-realist styles. In these ways they were, relatively belatedly, catching up on advances in European theatre production of earlier decades. Subsequent innovations, particularly associated with Patrice Chéreau and Harry Kupfer, have aroused hostility, unmodified by any sense of Bayreuth as an appropriate place for theatrical innovation.

A final attempt may be made to draw up a balance sheet. In terms of musical form, the continuity of thematic development achieved by Wagner's work would have emerged elsewhere; it is already apparent in the music of Brahms. Mythic subjects, associations between traditional myth and modern psychology, and anti-rationalism would all have become powerful forces in operatic, as in dramatic writing, had Wagner never lived. The anti-Semitism which rightly blackens Wagner's reputation as a thinker was not uniquely associated with him; Hitler did not need to hear and love Wagner in order to plan the annihilation of European Jewry.

A number of theatrical innovations may be associated with Wagner – the introduction of the darkened stage, the placing of the orchestra in an invisible pit, the practice of detailed gestural directing for individual singers and actors, and (in the purely orchestral sphere) a style of radically interpretative conducting. All of these practices have left their mark on the theatrical and musical history of the last hundred years.

Within Wagner's creative output, images of heroism – above all of heroic love – and conflicts between countervailing images of heroism are the most abiding legacy. Views of the composer as by rights an intellectual with responsibilities to all arts, not merely to music, and notions that every opera requires its own theory (imposing upon composers the duty of theoretical improvisation), prevalent and even commonplace today, can probably also be ascribed in their origins to Wagner. In these senses all twentieth-century opera is unthinkable without him. Of contemporary composers, Luciano Berio, John Adams, Michael Tippett and perhaps above all the German, Hans Werner Henze, have explicitly encountered Wagner's work and sought to appropriate, misappropriate and generally digest it as part as their own creative output.

Ultimately, Wagnerism rests on a certain type of appeal to a theatre audience. Wagner's notion of the *Gesamtkunstwerk* seems to postulate the evolution of an audience entirely integrated with itself. And his overall achievement certainly indicates how powerful can be the movements of consciousness initiated in spectators and listeners by musical theatre. But Wagner's work, as the analyses in this book have sought to show, constantly presents audiences with anomalies and discontinuities of mode. It does this above all and supremely in the *Ring*, by presenting fictive characters who are also symbols embodying objects, concepts and even contemporary allusions. In these ways Wagner's drama inherits the German tradition most remarkably embodied in Goethe's *Faust*. (My understanding of this is deeply indebted to the remarkable book by Benjamin Bennett, *Goethe's Theory of Poetry*.)

An audience that grasps such a mode of presentation is necessarily alienated, diverted from any straightforward involvement with the characters and implied assumptions of the drama. But, at the same time, it is enabled to attach additional significance to the spectacle which it confronts. The extent to which such extra meanings are grasped will vary, with the varying and overlapping social groups into which theatre audiences fall, and into which they perceive themselves, as a whole and in the various segments, as falling.

Such audiences, despite Wagnerian theory, will then necessarily be at odds with each other, in ways determined and provided for in advance by Wagnerian practice. What none the less draws any single audience together is precisely the conflictual mode of attention each of Wagner's works, to different degrees, requires. At its best, Wagner's musical drama achieves coherence by its sustained appeal, not to factitious social or psychological unity, but to self-critical emotional intelligence.

Selected Bibliography

There are countless books on Wagner. I have listed here a few of those which I have found helpful, together with books referred to in my own text.

Bennett, B., *Goethe's Theory of Poetry*, Cornell University, Press, Ithaca and London, 1986

Burbidge, P. and Sutton, R. (editors), *The Wagner Companion*, London, 1979

Cooke, D., *I Saw the World End: a study of Wagner's 'Ring'*, London, 1979

Dahlhaus, C., *The Music Dramas of Richard Wagner*, Cambridge, 1979

Deathridge, J. and Dahlhaus, C., *The New Grove Wagner*, London 1984

Gutman, R., *Richard Wagner: the man, his mind, and his music*, London 1968

Mann, T. (translated by Blunden, A.), *Pro and Contra Wagner*, London 1985

Millington, B., *Wagner*, London (2nd edition) 1992

Millington, B., *The Wagner Compendium. A guide to Wagner's life and music*, London 1992

Millington, B. and Spencer, S. (editors), *Wagner in Performance*, New Haven 1992

Murdoch, I., *Metaphysics as a Guide to Morals*, London 1992

Shaw, G. B., *The Perfect Wagnerite: a commentary on The Niblung's Ring*, New York 1967

Skelton, G., *Wagner at Bayreuth. Experiment and Tradition*, London (2nd edition) 1976

Skelton, G., *Wagner in Thought and Practice*, London 1991

Taylor, R., *Richard Wagner: his life, art and thought*, London 1979

Cosima Wagner's Diaries (translated by Skelton, G.), London 1978-80

Selected Letters of Richard Wagner (translated and edited by Spencer, S. and Millington, B.), London 1987

Wagner, R., *My Life* (translated by Gray, A., edited by Whittall, M.), Cambridge 1983

Richard Wagner's prose works (edited and translated by Ellis, W. A.), London 1892-99, reprinted 1972

Index

159